Western Lane

Western Lane

CHETNA MAROO

PICADOR INDIA

First published 2023 by Farrar, Straus and Giroux
120 Broadway, New York, NY 10271
First published in the UK 2023 by Picador
First published in paperback in India 2023 by Picador India
an imprint of Pan Macmillan Publishing India Private Limited
707 Kailash Building
26 K. G. Marg, New Delhi 110001
www.panmacmillan.co.in

Pan Macmillan, The Smithson, 6 Briset Street, Farringdon, London EC1M 5NR
Associated companies throughout the world
www.panmacmillan.com

ISBN 978-81-19300-15-0

1 3 5 7 9 8 6 4 2

Typeset by Palimpsest Book Production Ltd, Falkirk, Stirlingshire

Printed and bound in India by Thomson Press India Ltd.

For Jot

One

I don't know if you have ever stood in the middle of a squash court – on the T – and listened to what is going on next door. What I'm thinking of is the sound from the next court of a ball hit clean and hard. It's a quick, low pistol-shot of a sound, with a close echo. The echo, which is the ball striking the wall of the court, is louder than the shot itself. This is what I hear when I remember the year after our mother died, and our father had us practising at Western Lane two, three, four hours a day. It must have been an evening session after school, the first time I noticed it. My legs were so tired I didn't know if I could keep going and I was just standing on the T with my racket head down, looking at the side wall that was smudged with the washed-out marks from all the balls that had skimmed its surface. I was supposed to serve, and my father would return with a drive and I would volley, and my father would drive, and I would volley, aiming always for the red service line on the front wall. My father was standing far back, waiting.

I knew from his silence that he wasn't going to move first, and all I could do was serve and volley or disappoint him. The smudges on the wall blurred one into the other and I thought that surely I would fall. That was when it started up. A steady, melancholy rhythm from the other court, the shot and its echo, over and over again, like some sort of deliverance. I could tell it was one person conducting a drill. And I knew who it was. I stood there, listening, and the sound poured into me, into my nerves and bones, and it was with a feeling of having been rescued that I raised my racket and served.

There were three of us, all girls. When Ma died, I was eleven, Khush was thirteen, Mona fifteen. We'd been playing squash and badminton twice a week ever since we were old enough to hold a racket, but it was nothing like the regime that came after. Mona said that all of it, the sprints and the ghosting and the three-hour drills, started when our aunt Ranjan told Pa that what we girls needed was exercise and discipline and Pa sat quiet and let her tell him what to do.

That was at the beginning of autumn. The weather had turned from unseasonably dry and warm to humid. The air was oppressive and the streets smelled of decomposing food. In this heat, a number of days after Ma's funeral, we had driven four hundred miles to Edinburgh to have a meal at our aunt's home to mark the end of our mourning period, and Aunt Ranjan told Pa we were wild.

We were right there in her kitchen with her and Pa when she said it. Mona was washing potatoes in the sink. Her head was bowed and her sleeves were pushed to her elbows because she wasn't just rinsing the mud away. She was really scrubbing. Her ponytail swung over one shoulder. Khush was peeling slowly, staring out of the window. I was at the table seeding pomegranates. Aunt Ranjan had scolded Khush for wearing her hair loose in the kitchen, and then she'd turned to me and pulled up half of the white cloth and put newspapers down so I wouldn't get juice on her new dining set. It was a beautiful set, waxed and dark.

From where I was sitting I could see the gulab jamun Aunt Ranjan had prepared early that same morning. The dark-golden balls of sponge were already soaked in sugar syrup and piled generously in a glass bowl at the end of the counter.

Aunt Ranjan saw me looking.

'Gopi,' she said.

I froze in place, blushing fiercely at the sound of my name.

Aunt Ranjan stood up. She positioned herself so that she blocked my view of the sweets. I didn't know why but it seemed important to me that I not shift my focus, that I make it seem as if I'd been looking at nothing all along.

'Wild,' Aunt Ranjan said a second time, her eyes still on me. 'And it is no secret.'

Then she turned to Pa, and it was true that he just sat there looking at nothing, saying nothing.

Aunt Ranjan waited.

'Well, I have said my piece,' she said at last. 'Now it is up to you.'

Pa raised his eyes to look at Aunt Ranjan for a moment, and there was a coolness in them that we were used to but Aunt Ranjan was not. Her cheeks reddened. The pressure cooker on the gas ring gave a thin, high whistle and the kitchen was suddenly warm with steam and the smell of overcooked lentils. Aunt Ranjan dabbed her forehead with a clean tea towel off the back of a chair.

'I told Charu,' she said. 'I am not blaming her, brother, but I am telling you it is not too late for your girls.'

It was quiet. And then my sister Mona crossed to the worktop, removed the pressure cooker from the ring, and banged it hard onto the granite counter. The bowl of gulab jamun at the far end juddered and Mona stood with her potato-muddied hands on the lid of Aunt Ranjan's pressure cooker, staring at Pa.

Aunt Ranjan turned off the taps that Mona had left running and went to her.

'Not like that, child,' she said to Mona.

Our uncle came in then, as if wandering into someone else's kitchen. Maybe he would have gone right through into his garden but he looked at Mona, then Pa, and stood in the middle of the floor for a few seconds before approaching the table and sitting down between Pa and me. We liked Uncle Pavan. He was Pa's younger brother and he was big and kind and enjoyed smoking outside and thinking about the past.

Uncle Pavan was forty. Pa was almost forty-five. But everyone talked about how handsome the brothers had become as if they had only lately grown into adulthood. After Ma died, our aunties' eyes followed Pa from the dinner table to the sink or out into the garden. They were sorry for him, but they were also trying to get the measure of something and we knew it had to do with the space that had opened out in front of him.

It wasn't yet midday and it was already too warm for Uncle Pavan. His face was glowing and pink as anything. He put a hand on the table, tapped his four fingers on the cloth, all at once, and then moved his hand to his thigh. He needed a smoke. He glanced at Pa and clasped his hands in his lap, ready to talk. Khush had poured Uncle Pavan a glass of water, and seeing he was ready she placed it on the table in front of him and sat down to hear what he had to say. Uncle Pavan gave her a grateful look and began.

'It was the middle of a heat wave,' he said. He leaned towards Pa. 'Do you remember? The night you told Bapuji you were getting married. You were out late and Bapuji insisted we all stay up for you. We had to put boxes of ice in front of the fans and we couldn't move, it was so hot. When you finally came home, Bapuji told you to come in and asked you in front of everyone what you thought you were doing. You didn't hesitate. You stood in the doorway and said it as if it was the most natural thing in the world. I am getting married. Like that. It was wonderful. I will never forget the look on Bapuji's face. You see . . . I . . . Charu . . . she was . . . she . . .'

Uncle Pavan seemed about to choke on something inside his throat, and we could see that Pa wanted him to keep talking, but Uncle Pavan couldn't.

'It is no use dwelling on things,' Aunt Ranjan said. She put a hand on Uncle Pavan's shoulder. 'Come, Pavan. Bring two more chairs from the garage so we can all sit together.'

By the time we sat down to eat, it was four o'clock. The air was heavy and close and everything moved slowly in it. Aunt Ranjan, Uncle Pavan, Pa and I waited at our places while my sisters served the dinner. We each had a silver plate, onto which my sisters placed a small silver bowl of dal, a whole ladu, potato shaak, rice, puris, a salad of onions and tomatoes, and a second silver bowl containing three gulab jamuns. Khush's hair kept sticking to her forehead and to her hot cheeks and she kept pushing it back. When I saw Khush spooning extra syrup on top of the jamuns in my bowl, her hair almost dipping in the syrup, I made myself look elsewhere.

The door into the garden was open. There was no breeze. Aunt Ranjan talked about her siblings in Tanzania who had too many children. She ate carefully, taking small mouthfuls at long intervals, and we tried to do the same. When I had finished everything on my plate apart from my three gulab jamuns, she looked at my full little bowl with all its syrup. I put down my spoon.

'Brother,' she said, turning to Pa, and I wanted to shout at her that Pa was not her brother, that Pa was Uncle Pavan's brother. 'Brother,' she said, 'a difficult time is coming for you.'

Uncle Pavan shuffled his chair closer to the table. 'Ranjan,' he murmured.

'No,' Aunt Ranjan told him. 'He understands.'

She looked at Pa and began to speak in Gujarati, keeping her voice low and even. What she said was that she and Uncle Pavan had no children, that they loved their brother and they loved us as if we were their own. She said it would be easier on Pa if he allowed them to take one of us. You cannot look after three, she said. Three is too many. And when Pa was silent, she took it as a sign to continue. She said, People do this. No one would have raised an eyebrow had you done this even when the girls' mother was alive. Then she said that her own sister had flown over two and a half thousand miles from Mombasa to Bombay to live with their aunt when she was younger than me, and we were only talking about a few hours in the car.

Pa was staring at his plate. He knew that we'd understood what Aunt Ranjan had said. That was why he didn't look at us. We thought that he would allow her words to sit for a moment so that she would see for herself how she had got things wrong, and then he would stand up and step out into the garden, telling us to get our things because we were leaving. But he didn't stand up, he didn't say anything, and in the end we were glad, because whatever Aunt Ranjan saw in his face frightened her more than any reply he could have made. Her own face turned grey and seemed to lose its firmness. When she picked up her glass of chaas to take a sip, her mouth sagged.

That was when Uncle Pavan's voice rose into the silence. It was slow and firm. Spring had come early this year. We should have seen the flowers on the horse chestnut tree. Like Christmas lights. And then there were the cherry blossoms: for one week, the whole lawn was white. We ate and Uncle Pavan talked, and one way or another things drifted into a rhythm that seemed ordinary. We felt a light breeze from the garden. Uncle Pavan wiped his hands on a cloth, stood up, and brought the gulab jamuns to the table to refill our bowls.

'Oh,' Aunt Ranjan said mournfully into her plate as we raised our spoons again. 'That day,' and she was crying. She took hold of the free end of her sari and touched her eyes with it. She turned her head to smile at Khush through the tears.

'I saw you,' she said, her voice lower still, claiming Khush, 'in the car park, after.'

She was talking about Ma's funeral, and Khush's crying silently when we were all lined up to greet our relatives as they came outside. Aunt Ranjan looked at Khush with such sadness that we forgot everything. Khush put her hand on the table between her own plate and Aunt Ranjan's. Next to me, Mona's chair scraped the floor badly, and I moved my hand towards my glass of chaas but the glass was tall and it toppled and the chaas spilled, spreading into the tablecloth.

'Gopi,' Aunt Ranjan murmured. I blushed again at my name being spoken aloud, but Aunt Ranjan was not scolding. Her face was fixedly serene as she stood, as she came around to lift the cloth and fold it in, as she saw the chaas had gone through onto her table. I sat there while she moved around me, wiping and rearranging things.

Whenever we were staying in the house in Edinburgh, we each had our own bedroom, but Khush and I always dragged our blankets into Mona's room and slept on the floor. We propped the French windows open with our trainers because there was usually something going on outside. We listened until we were tired, and then we dreamed. That night, it was too warm for sleep. We were restless and sweating in our shorts and vest tops. We thrust our blankets off us and then we were nothing but hot, damp limbs; legs and arms thrown out any which way to try to get cool. Khush pushed herself up and went out onto the balcony. I followed. Outside, Khush reclined, half lying on the tiles, half leaning against one side of the window frame, a skinny arm stretched out across the floor, and I positioned myself the same way on the other side. But after a while we both sat up with our chins on our knees and stared through the white balustrades into the garden. Since it was too warm for leggings or sleeves, I stank of citronella and got bitten by mosquitoes anyway. We knew that Pa would be getting bitten too. He and Uncle Pavan were talking outside. They were sitting right under our balcony, drinking whisky and smoking. Pa didn't drink or smoke at home, but he liked to when he was with Uncle Pavan. We could see the blue smoke from Uncle's cigarettes and hear their talk and the clink of their glasses. We could hear everything, even the creak of Pa's chair as he bent to lift or lower his glass or scratch at his ankle. And when we looked out we could see everything they saw: Uncle's rose arbour and his trees and the stone bench and glimpses of the railway track, grainy and dark.

It didn't matter to us what they talked about. Childhood remembrances of themselves and of their younger brother, who died early. The three of them playing racket sports. The three of them eager and happy. Pa surprising everyone because he, so mild, so unassuming in life, was brutal on the court. And later when Ma came along – seventeen, bright-eyed, self-conscious – Pa finding himself at a loss, touched by something he couldn't name. Uncle Pavan did most of the talking and Pa let him know that he had things about right. It didn't matter to us. We just wanted to sit above them and listen. Afterwards, when Pa and Uncle finished up and went inside, we stayed out. The morning light was beginning to come up by then, a pale transparent blue, and the air was cooler and everything outside seemed close enough to touch. Khush's hair was loose so that it came down her back in soft waves and even in this light, it shone. We didn't go in until I started shivering. We pulled the doors closed behind us. Inside, we climbed onto Mona's bed. Mona grouched at being woken, but she shifted and we got in close under her blanket, and told her everything. It was Khush who did the telling. When something happened, even if everyone was there, it was always Khush who would tell it. She'd wait until we fell silent, and begin. She was good at telling. She remembered things we didn't think of.

Much later, Khush would say that that night was really the start of it, of Pa's thinking about what he would do with us. It wasn't Aunt Ranjan. It was Uncle Pavan talking about the past. But I think Pa told us himself what moved him. He sat beside us one morning on the bench outside the squash court and said, 'I want you to become interested in something you can do your whole life.'

Aunt Ranjan had orange juice and pancakes with lemon and sugar ready on the table for us in the morning. She said nothing about Pa and Uncle Pavan sitting out drinking and smoking all night. She made them coffee and stood near them so she could refill their cups. Pa spoke kindly to her. Outside in the driveway when Uncle Pavan was closing the door of the car boot over our luggage, Aunt Ranjan asked Pa to think about what she had suggested, and he said he would. She said that she and Uncle Pavan would come to our house next year. We will know how things are by then, she said.

Pa began our regime as soon as we returned home from Edinburgh. During the week, he drove us to Western Lane before school, and we got the bus there after school. On weekends, if Pa had work we rode our bikes and he joined us when he was done. We needed rest days at first because everything hurt so much: arms, legs, shoulders. Everything. Pa told us we would get used to it, and we did. Before long we could hardly remember when we used to play only once or twice a week as if it was for fun.

The courts at Western Lane were often empty. Men from the Vauxhall factory came most Saturdays, and most of them thrashed about, running at the ball and smashing it as hard as possible. My sisters and I would sit on one of the benches outside the courts in our sweatshirts and tracksuit bottoms and wait for them to finish before going in and starting our drills. Apart from the Vauxhall men there were a few occasional players, and then there was Ged.

Ged was thirteen and quiet and his real name was Gethen. He spent a lot of time at Western Lane because his mother worked in the bar upstairs and he had nowhere else he preferred to be. Since the summer, Ged had grown quite tall and he was awkward with it, except when he was on court. On court there was a looseness about him. It was in the way he moved, but it wasn't only that. He practised by himself and I watched him from the balcony sometimes. Once, when he and I were at the far end of the balcony looking down to the swimming pool, I asked him did he mind my watching, and he looked at me for a moment and then he looked at the swimming pool and said no.

Most people only came to Western Lane for the swimming pool. It had a diving board and a deep end. But we came for the courts. Pa paid for membership that allowed us to use the courts any time between 7:30 a.m. and 10:00 p.m. as long as we booked in advance. It didn't matter to Pa that the paint on the walls was peeling or the floor needed sanding or the air-conditioning rarely worked: the courts at Western Lane had glass backs.

There was also the bar. Pa went up there sometimes in the same suit he wore to work and to the sports centre and everywhere and though he didn't drink or say much, people talked to him and they liked him. Sometimes they found out he worked for himself as an electrician, and at first he got more work that way because they asked him to come to their homes to look at their fridges or their heating, but after a while when they asked him would he come, he said he would be glad to come soon, it was just that he was quite busy right now, and then he would excuse himself and get us each a bottle of Coke from the bar, and while we drank he would look at his own Coke bottle and talk to us about Jahangir Khan, a young player from Pakistan – a boy – who had become the world number one. It wasn't Jahangir, Pa explained, but Jahangir's older brother, Torsam, who was supposed to be the champion. This brother died when Jahangir was fifteen, and Jahangir began to train with his cousin Rahmat in Wembley. Rahmat both pushed Jahangir and looked after him. He took Jahangir to the mountains, to the Khyber Pass, to remind him where he had come from and who he was. Jahangir was still only a boy when, two years after his brother's death, he won the World Open Championship. And for five years after that, in which time he played five hundred and fifty-five matches, Jahangir Khan was unbeaten. Five hundred and fifty-five matches played without a single loss, Pa said, and we too stared at Pa's Coke bottle while we drank from ours.

I remember one Saturday in particular. We had cycled to Western Lane after our Gujarati class. The Vauxhall men weren't there. Ged was on one of the courts and when he saw we'd arrived, he acknowledged us and continued with his practice. We sat on the bench and looked into our court, which was empty. I don't know what we were thinking. We were tired from our week, I suppose. All the doors were open and the sound of people in the swimming pool was loud and echoing, and upstairs we could hear Ged's mother vacuuming the bar. She left the vacuum on while she moved tables around. Pa came, and we didn't hear him at first, so he had time to observe us sitting doing nothing with an empty court in front of us. He positioned his bag on the end of our bench.

We got our rackets and went into the court, and Pa stood in his suit facing us from the other side of the glass. He didn't go to change into his training things. He didn't instruct us. The white notebook in which he usually wrote the details of our drills lay unopened on the bench behind him. We understood that he wanted us to train by ourselves and so we did a few sprints and then practised our drives. While one of us practised, the other two stood at the front of the court. After several minutes of watching Khush and then me trying to hit the ball along the wall, Mona dropped her racket, removed a trainer, and put it down as a target for us, between the service box and the back wall on the forehand side. We didn't push ourselves. We played the same stroke over and over and then nudged Mona's trainer forwards or back and did the same again, which was what Pa would have had us do, but when we made ourselves do it, time dragged, and the whole thing felt laborious.

While Khush was driving for the fifth or sixth time with the ball dying in the service box, I joined Mona at the front of the court. Because Khush seemed so slight and delicate you might think she wouldn't be able to hit at all, but she could hit. She was just tired. Her legs were tired. Mona's gaze was fixed on Pa and I suppose that after a while mine was too. And then there were three of us as Khush, bending to retrieve the ball, came up staring at him.

Pa's face, his whole body, was so empty of expression that we were embarrassed. He didn't notice we had stopped, and we understood we were probably intruding on something private. We kept staring. I don't know what made me step towards Pa, or what it was I thought I was going to do. I felt Khush tap the head of her racket against mine. She passed me the ball and took her place next to Mona.

Something cool, like ice, began to expand inside my chest. I thought of snow, white everywhere. I moved into position and hit the ball. I wasn't thinking of hitting. I was thinking of the boy Jahangir Khan charging through the snow in the mountains of northern Pakistan, and of someone standing far off in the frozen landscape, watching him. Even from some distance, the water in the boy's breath could be seen freezing quickly in the air as if it was still part of him. My racket accelerated and I felt Pa's eyes on me. I was hitting well. There was air in my movement. I was breathing easily, bringing my shoulder round, hitting the ball deep.

I had been on for less than a minute when Mona said, 'That's enough.'

She stood at the front of the court with one shoe on, looking at Pa.

Pa neither acknowledged nor contradicted her and so we warmed down, then came out and sat on the bench. Pa remained where he was.

'We don't have our towels,' Mona said.

Pa didn't reply. She said it again.

That was when Pa began talking quietly into the empty court. At first he was talking about Jahangir Khan's family: Jahangir's father, Roshan Khan, and uncles Hashim and Azam Khan, who between the three of them won the World Open twelve times, his uncle Nasrullah Khan, his brother, Torsam, his cousin and coach Rahmat. The whole dynasty. But at some point we must have stopped listening because suddenly he was no longer talking about the Khans, but about an Australian player named Geoff Hunt who beat his own brother to win a state championship at the age of fifteen and went on to dominate the game for almost a decade. A generation of Pakistanis were unable to overcome Hunt, Pa said. He was too fit. It didn't matter how brilliant the Pakistanis were if they couldn't even get to the ball. And then Jahangir came along and he saw what he would be up against and he got fit, and he beat Hunt.

'Because you have to have something.' Pa's voice was so strange and unlike his voice that we had to concentrate to understand him. 'You have to address yourself to something,' he said.

Mona fixed her eyes on Pa.

'We're not Khans,' she murmured.

Pa came to the bench and bent down to put his notebook inside his bag.

'We're brothers,' he said. 'Indians and Pakistanis.'

Mona didn't answer. There was enough hostility in her face without putting it into words, and Pa saw it. It wasn't because of anything he had done. It was because he had not forced us to do anything. It was because we had spent an hour in the court of our own free will, and we would do it again tomorrow.

At home in the evenings, I'd wonder aloud, Would Ged be at Western Lane this whole time, would he be there until the early hours of the morning when the last person left the bar and we were sleeping?

'Don't worry,' Khush would reply.

We'd be bent over the sink in the bathroom brushing our teeth. Khush would keep pushing my hair away from my face as well as hers. On the morning of Ma's funeral, we had cut my hair into a bob and it was too short and choppy to stay tucked behind my ears.

We'd raise our heads and regard one another in the mirror. Khush's face was pretty. Heart-shaped and open. Everything was close to the surface with her. In this way you could say she was like Uncle Pavan. When she was moved, her eyes filled with tears. She sweated instantly when she was hot. People said I was most like Ma because I had Ma's gestures and expressions, and I supposed this was what Khush was looking for when she searched my face in the mirror. But when you are very close to two people, it is hard to see how they are alike.

'Things are going to be okay,' she'd say.

'I know,' I'd reply, and we'd spit into the sink and turn the taps.

We broke from school for our half-term holiday in October. Mona was almost constantly angry with Pa by then, but when she wasn't, she was religious about going visiting with him. Pa went visiting most Sunday afternoons. It was what he and Ma had always done when Ma was alive. He liked us to go along, but he never forced us.

Visiting meant sitting for half an hour or an hour at the house of an uncle or aunt or distant cousin, and then another and another, or if there was someone our parents knew who was sick in hospital it meant going there instead. When Ma was alive, and an aunt or older cousin had found out that Mona had been seen in town with a group of friends that included boys, or that Khush and I had come home from school with scratches or bruises on our skin or rips in our uniforms, they would shake their heads at us and tell us to think about Ma, as if she wasn't sitting right there beside us.

Now, depending on where he went, Pa could usually fit three or four visits into an afternoon. He said you had to keep in touch with people, and we ought to try a bit. We watched his face, and we could see his heart wasn't in this. And so we said we didn't know these people. And he said you have to make an effort if you want to know someone.

We were making an effort with each other, we said, and stayed home.

On the first Sunday of our holiday, Mona went with Pa, and Khush and I went to the fort behind our house. The fort was three brick walls around a cement floor. The side walls were high and graduated. We thought that someone taller than us could have climbed up to the first level if they could get a good enough foothold and from there they could climb to the very top. It was amazing to us that none of the children nearby went in there. We were the only ones. No one spat on us from a height or told us to go home. No one ran us out of there. No one came near. In the summer we spent hours in the fort, hitting a tennis ball against the back wall or just sitting around.

When Ma was alive, we used to watch Wimbledon on TV and eat strawberries covered in sugar, all of us together, and then my sisters and I would come out to the fort and pretend to be John McEnroe. Khush did him best. She got the speech and the walk perfectly. Though we loved and admired him, we were bewildered that both Ma and Pa did too. We were only children, but even we could see that he was acting spoiled. Pa said that maybe he didn't know it himself, but with his complaining and tantrums, John McEnroe was making a space for himself, giving himself time, and in that time he was situating himself in such a way that the world was against him, and the only choice he had was to come out fighting. What amazed me was that John McEnroe could come away from the umpire's chair with his shoulders slumped and his whole body depressed, and then lift his racket and play the way he played. I thought his body was tricking his mind in some way.

In front of the open section of the fort was a grass-covered hill as tall as our house. To the right, a block of flats, five storeys, with red and yellow cladding and walkways that kids flew along on their bikes and skateboards. Opposite, the main road with the bus stop and the underpass we avoided.

I had Khush's tennis racket and was bouncing a ball on its strings up and down a thousand times. We were trying not to think of anything. When Pa had been readying to leave with Mona that morning, he had pulled his car keys from his coat and then stopped in the middle of the kitchen. He had looked at each one of us – Mona next to him, dressed and ready to go, Khush at one end of the empty table, and me at the other – and in those few seconds we saw that he perceived his situation plainly. Had he spoken then, we imagined, it would have been to say: I didn't want this. What he saw was the days stretching ahead of him without Ma, with us. It was part of our training, the bouncing of the ball on the racket or the floor. Keep your eye on the ball, Pa told us. I liked doing it and might have kept on, but Khush became tired of watching me. I put the racket down and we sat against the back wall of the fort wrapped snugly in our coats and scarves, facing the hill, talking about what we'd do over the holidays. Pa would be working, which meant that once we'd done our chores, we could laze about in the mornings until it was time to go to Western Lane and after that we'd be free to do what we wanted. On Saturday, since there would be no Gujarati school, we'd train early, and afterwards if Pa wasn't tired we might have an outing somewhere. Our Tanzania cousins who had been scheduled to visit us had cancelled because of Ma. They thought it would be too much for Pa to cope with by himself. Had they come to us, we would have taken them to Woburn Safari Park. Whenever we had visitors from India or Africa, we packed the boot of our car with Tupperware boxes filled with curries and onion salad and parathas, and drove our guests up the M1 to see the lions. Khush acted as if the whole dumb idea made her crazy, but she loved it as much as I did. We loved the animals. We loved driving around the big park. We loved watching our relatives trying so hard to be impressed by it in front of Ma and Pa and all of us. Since our cousins weren't coming, we would go, instead, to Dunstable Downs or the Tree Cathedral.

The sun was shining into the fort and our faces were lit up and pleasantly warm.

I was trying to discuss what it meant to be wild, in Aunt Ranjan's account of things. Usually we made lists. Wearing shorts if you were a girl. Running indoors. Running anywhere. Sticking your elbows out of car windows. But Khush wasn't joining in. She was just sitting there, letting me talk. I stopped. We looked out at the hill.

Khush said, 'Aunt Ranjan's afraid of us because she doesn't know how to find out what we're thinking.'

I wanted to ask Khush what had been going on with her lately. She had become preoccupied and she wasn't listening to her radio or reading or anything like that. But the main thing was her getting out of bed at night, staying up in the dark on the landing outside our bedroom. Mona and I would lie still and listen to her. We weren't sure, but it sounded to us like Khush was trying to get to Ma. She was talking in Gujarati. We could tell this despite not being able to hear the words. We had always spoken to Pa and our aunts and uncles in English but never to Ma because, though she understood English, it was hard for her. And our Gujarati wasn't enough. That was why we had always listened to Ma so closely, and watched her. Maybe it was why we pulled at her, pushed into her, made ourselves physical in her presence. Khush had been out there, on the landing, every few nights since we came back from Edinburgh.

I wanted to ask Khush about Ma, and whether she really thought Ma might be able to hear what she was saying out on the landing. But we were happy, the two of us, sitting with the sun on us, and so I didn't ask her anything.

Khush removed her gloves, put them in her pockets.

'Ged's okay, isn't he?' she said after a minute.

'What?'

She turned to face me. She said shyly, 'Do you like him?'

I looked at her, and all of a sudden I felt depressed.

'He's okay,' I said.

The sun started going down behind the hill, and then it got cold fast. The hill and the flats lost their colour and a silence settled on the estate. In the cold, colourless gloom we saw the dog Fourth Avenue coming out of the shadows behind the hill, yellow-dog-teeth bared, shoulders lurching from side to side. We'd named Fourth Avenue for the direction from which he always approached, although sometimes it just seemed that one minute he wasn't there and the next minute he was. He was big and dark. He walked around the estate taking his time, with his big lousy head moving slowly and his tongue red and awful. He was awful, not of this world. One of us must have been saying something, but whoever it was stopped. We waited. Fourth Avenue came around the hill and began walking across the fort's entrance like a brute, like he had nowhere to be, and the whole estate was his. His shoulders moved slowly and when he was level with us and the sounds of our beating hearts must have been in his ears, he turned his head and looked at Khush, dead on – one eye yellow, the other watery and dark as anything – and then he glanced away and moved on.

Khush kept her hand on mine to steady me, but I kept shaking. The way Fourth Avenue had looked at Khush, it was as if she was wherever he was. I wanted to go inside but we had to wait because Fourth Avenue would wander around the block, past the front of our house before going up towards the school.

'He saw you,' I whispered.

Khush pulled her scarf up over her mouth.

'We can go inside now,' she said through the wool, once he was out of sight.

We walked slowly past the backs of the houses in our street. At home, Khush opened the fridge and asked me did I want Coke and I said not really, and went into the garden. I stayed out until Pa and Mona returned home. Mona opened the door into the garden and I thought she would call me in, but she just stood there for a minute and then left the door ajar and went back into the kitchen. I followed. Mona wasn't talking to Pa. She was wandering about restlessly and when I asked her where she and Pa had gone, she said, 'Nowhere,' and switched the radio on. Khush was in the living room flicking between channels on the TV. At 8.00 p.m. the sound on both the TV and the radio shot up and then immediately cut out. The silence, coming after the sudden noise, was terrible. Khush came into the kitchen, ready to ask what we had done, but once she saw our faces she didn't bother. She went to bed early. It started raining hard. It was an awful evening, everyone on edge, and I didn't know why and maybe no one else did either.

At 2.00 a.m., when we should have been sleeping, we were all wide awake. Mona and I were lying still in our bunks, because we were listening – through our blankets and the noise of the radiator and the rain and the thick, wet branches of the plum tree knocking against our bedroom window – to Khush, out on the landing, talking to Ma. Her voice was dark and whispering and anxious and it made us anxious too. Pa's room was next door, and we knew he must hear her. We knew that if we went to the landing, we would discover her backed against the end of the banister where we'd all loaded our coats, and that if we went out to get her, she would return with us to her bed. But no one went to get her. She was out there, talking and listening, and it seemed to us that something was getting through.

We heard her come back into the bedroom close to 6.00 a.m. Khush knew her way around the beds and all our things on the floor, or else she had become used to the dark. She didn't bang a knee on a bedpost or trip over a racket or a rucksack or anything else. She climbed under her blanket and lay there until an hour later, when everyone was up around her and she got up too.

I told Khush she could take my place in the queue for the bathroom. While I waited, I stood next to the radiator in the bedroom, trying to find a hot section. Air had been trapped inside our radiators for more than a month, which meant that big sections were cold and the house never got properly warm. My sisters and I dressed in long sleeves and hooded tops and said nothing to Pa. In the past, Pa would have fixed the problem right away, but now he ignored it. Mona came and stood next to me. It wasn't just the warmth we were seeking. We wanted to feel the knocking as we stood against the radiator. We understood the knocking was only the air trapped inside. We wanted to feel it.

When Khush came out of the bathroom, I went in. I put down the toilet lid and sat waiting for the hot water tank to fill up. I felt that it should have been me out on the landing. And I knew Mona was feeling that it should have been her.

The bathroom was colder than the bedroom. The light blue paint on the walls was peeling in places and one of the tiles above the bath was loose. The summer before I entered junior school, we had spent a whole week preparing and painting the walls, and we were ecstatic the first time we had people over who would see it. They were coming for my seventh birthday. On the morning of my birthday I was sitting as I was now, on the toilet with the lid down, and Ma was standing next to me doing her hair in the mirror, and Khush and Mona were crowded in there too, perched on the edge of the bath. We had the door closed. Everything smelled new and we were happy. Ma had to keep wiping the mirror with the edge of her hand because it kept misting up. After she'd brushed her hair and twisted it into a knot, she got her sindoor out of the cabinet. It was in a tiny, flat copper container, and the powder was bright red. Vermilion, Khush said. Ma dabbed her finger in the powder and made a vermilion line in her parting, all the way along.

Can I have it? I whispered. That was what I meant to say, but I only knew how to say, Will you give it to me?

Ma laughed and touched my cheek. After your wedding, she said.

When Ma went downstairs, Khush made me stay seated, and she got the powder from the cabinet and dabbed her finger just as Ma had done, and she came close and made a line in my parting. Then she touched my cheek the same way Ma had done and she said, 'Happy birthday.'

And I went downstairs like that. Aunt Ranjan was there and Uncle Pavan and everyone else. Ma had to turn her face to the window to hide her smile. Khush saw that Ma liked it and she was encouraged even though Aunt Ranjan kept saying it was bad luck. Khush ran up to get Ma's red wedding veil. She put it over my head to make me a bride. Pa had placed a stool in the middle of the room for my cake, and Khush made me walk seven times around the stool as if it was a wedding fire, and then she paraded me up and down, introducing me to my new in-laws. When she brought me finally to Pa, he looked first at me in Ma's veil and then at Ma, and he too had to turn his face to the window and it wasn't to hide anything, it was because the living room was too small to hold what he felt. It was Khush who remembered that about Pa. All that I remembered of my seventh birthday was circling the living room and seeing everything through Ma's red veil, but Khush had told me the story of the whole day after the funeral, when we saw our aunties going through Ma's things and one of them took Ma's sindoor.

I stood up to look in the mirror. I ran my finger along my parting and when the hot water was ready I washed my face. I took my time getting showered and dressed. I just wanted to look clean and nice, in case.

Pa had already left for work and there were still two hours before we had to leave for Western Lane. In the bedroom, Mona was at the dressing table. Khush's bed was made and her bedclothes were on her pillow, neatly folded. When I went outside, I found her sitting on the doorstep. She was wearing Pa's ulster coat with its massive cape. The sleeves were rolled up and I could see that when she stood, the hem would drag along the floor. There was a layer of frost on top of the wall opposite and on the ground and the doorstep.

'What you doing?'

She looked up and smiled. 'You look nice.'

I brushed some of the frost off the doorstep with the edge of my boot and sat down next to her. 'Thank you.'

Her fingers were blue with the cold and when she saw me looking at them she slipped her hands inside her pockets.

'Khush,' I said, 'what was she saying to you?'

I thought she wasn't going to answer, but after a minute, she said, 'Who?'

'Ma.'

'Oh.' She stood up, lifting the hem of Pa's coat by raising her hands inside the pockets. 'She wasn't saying anything.'

'But she was on the landing?'

She looked at me. 'It's not like that,' she said.

'What is it like?' I said.

And even as I said it I felt something I hardly had hold of slipping away because, after all, I knew there was nothing. It was just Khush, on the landing by herself, trying to get somewhere.

'It's okay,' I said. 'You don't have to say.'

Khush sat down again and looked at the garages opposite, and the alleyway into Arrow Close. She took her hands out of her pockets and they were still blue with cold. Suddenly I wanted to explain to her about Ged. I had got upset at her when she'd asked me about him before and I was sorry, but I still didn't know what to say, exactly. Something to do with the time he taped my racket for me. Or his stammer. You had to be quiet and let him get his words out and, sometimes, in the middle of a sentence, there would be nothing, and it might only be for a moment, but you could feel him trying, and it seemed like you were drifting closer to him in the silence, when you hadn't moved at all. I looked at Khush's profile. She would have known what to say about Ged. I wanted to go back inside. Khush didn't move. She had her hands on the doorstep, her fingers so blue and frozen that the tips of my own fingers burned.

Two

The movement around a squash court isn't like any other movement. From the T to the back of the court, there's a way of pivoting sideways, a positive move and then a sort of drifting. After you strike the ball, the momentum of the strike drives you back up the court, and it's better if you don't arrive late or too early. At the same time, you mustn't worry about arriving late or too early because worrying about it will only make you wrong-foot yourself. Ghosting is a way of grooving the movement. You make the movements of the game with the racket but without the ball, over and over, inside the court.

When we ghosted, Pa would stand at the front of the court, instructing us. He would indicate with his hand in order to convey which shot we were to ghost next. A drop to the forehand corner, a backhand volley, a straight drive. He varied the time between one instruction and the next. We might barely have recovered from a drop before he'd bring us back to the same corner, and then the same again, and then again, or he might hold us too long at the T, breaking our momentum. He wouldn't let us know in advance how long the rally would last.

Sometimes he instructed us from the balcony, and instead of indicating our shots he called numbers, each number corresponding with a section of the court. He never raised his voice. The whole thing created a disorienting awareness of the court not only from the ground, but from above. We would feel our thoughts slipping into his, and then it would seem to us that we wouldn't have to listen at all, because we knew our next move at the same moment he did.

Pa wrote to his childhood friend Bala in Mombasa to tell him about Ma's passing. Bala wrote back and they began corresponding regularly. On Friday evenings when it was dark out, Pa would sit at the kitchen table under the tube light and write for ninety minutes before addressing an envelope, slipping the pages inside and leaving it by the door for morning. We would be doing something else, homework, or ironing, or reading, but we were always aware of him sitting there. Pa's face was alert when he was writing to his friend. He was completely present elsewhere, not in our kitchen with us. Before Diwali, instead of a letter, Pa got a package from Bala, and it was addressed to me and my sisters as well as to him. Pa let me open it. Inside was a video: three hours of Jahangir Khan. The video became part of our training.

In the fortnight running up to Diwali it was freezing outside and we watched the video almost every night with the curtains open and the feeling that there was snow coming. Usually we went to Edinburgh for Diwali, and Uncle Pavan lit fireworks in his garden. We liked Uncle's display and the big potatoes he baked on his fire. We even liked helping him clear away the spent fireworks and paper debris in his garden the following morning. But this time none of us wanted to go.

We brought our suitcases down from the loft after school. Mona cancelled the weekend's milk and we all sat in the living room with the sky darkening outside and the TV on. Maybe Pa could feel that we needed something from him. He muted the TV and sat forward as if he was listening for some tiny sound. We held our breath. Pa pushed himself up from the sofa and put a hand to my forehead. He let it sit there and looked right into my eyes, until all I could see were the dark depths of his, and then he went out to the hall to telephone Aunt Ranjan.

He told Aunt Ranjan I was getting a fever and we had better stay home.

Khush pulled a blanket up to her chin and kept her eyes on the TV, and so did Mona. We listened to Pa talking in the hall, answering questions about my appetite and temperature. Mona reached over for the remote. She turned the sound up. When Pa returned, he sat down and clasped his hands between his knees.

'It is better this way,' he told us.

Mona leaned into Pa on the sofa while Khush and I moved to the floor and lay on our stomachs on the carpet and then sat up with our backs against their knees. We sat like this for a long time with the flickering light of the TV on us.

In the days that followed, my sisters and I settled into new routines. In the fort we hit tennis balls against the front wall, and when Mona or Khush hit a ball out of the fort I fetched it. At home, we watched Bala's video with Pa. I sat near the TV because I was the one who would stop and rewind the video when Pa wanted to show us something. There was a line between us, Mona and Khush on one side, me on the other.

Sometimes Pa asked me what I thought he wanted us to notice. If I hesitated, he sat forward and said, 'Think it out,' and if I answered correctly, he let his gaze rest on me and sat back in his chair, a thoughtful expression on his face, and my sisters watched him.

It was around this time that Mona, who had become increasingly touchy and achy and prone to headaches and bad moods, began speculating which one of us Pa was most likely to offer up to Aunt Ranjan. She looked at me in the dressing table mirror.

'You don't need to worry about anything as long as you stay exactly as you are right now,' she said. She placed her comb on the dressing table next to her bottle of coconut oil.

Days later, when we were sitting with our homework on the upper floor of the Marsh Farm Library, Mona leaned across the table and whispered loudly that my breasts were beginning to show.

I kept my head lowered over my books. My hands became hot. I felt a sudden violence in my body.

Someone said, 'Shh.' Mona gathered her books and went and sat elsewhere.

On the morning of Diwali we woke in our own beds and went downstairs. It was still dark. Mona unwrapped the glass swans we used for our Diwali lights. Ma had tried to teach us to fill the swans' bodies with coloured water. We had to tip them in a particular way in order to get the water into the necks and heads, and then float a candle on each swan's back. Ma usually ended up making my swan for me. Mona handed me a swan, and I felt her and Khush watching me. I tried to give it back.

'You do it,' I said.

'No.'

I put my hand inside the water jug to remove the red crepe paper we had used for dye, and poured the now translucent red water from the jug into the glass swan. I tipped and righted the swan, lengthened the wick of the candle, and floated the candle in the water. When I had finished, Mona put the red swan next to the sink and we all three looked at it. There was a long air bubble floating in the curve of the swan's neck. The swan's head looked as if it was unconnected to its body.

'I'll try again,' I said.

'Why?' Mona said. 'We don't have time.'

She and Khush made their swans and then we took them into the living room and placed them in a row on the wall unit, and when Pa came downstairs Mona showed him which swan belonged to each of us.

Since we hadn't gone to Aunt Ranjan's for Diwali, we would go on Christmas Eve. We would drive to Edinburgh in the morning and return home the following evening. And on Boxing Day we would visit people Pa knew in town.

I started waking at 6.00 a.m. because I could be alone then. In the week before Christmas, when everything was grey and it was raining heavily outside, I was crouched in front of the TV in the living room in my leggings and sweatshirt while everyone was asleep upstairs. Bala's video was playing.

Something happens when you watch three hours of Jahangir Khan. You start to believe that he is reading his opponents' minds. Jahangir is fit and quick and he's graceful, but it's the way he follows his opponent's thoughts that makes you keep watching. He can play whatever game his opponent is playing, use their weapons against them, or else blow away all opposition with his own. In each game, it's the same Jahangir, but not the same. It's as if something is modulated to give him the advantage over Hiddy Jahan or Gogi Alauddin or Qamar Zaman or Geoff Hunt or whoever he's up against. The players know what they are about to face, and they are completely in the dark.

The sound was muted. I was trying to see what Pa saw, in case it was something different from what I saw. Pa never talked about Jahangir reading anyone's mind. He talked about the feeling that Jahangir had for a situation, his sense for what was going on behind him.

I heard someone coming downstairs and going into the kitchen and after a few minutes, Khush came in with a plate of digestive biscuits with slices of orange arranged on top. It was what Ma used to bring us. I turned the sound up.

Khush preferred the players who made something spectacular out of the game, who could swing the racket as though they were about to crack the ball to the back of the court, only to open their racket face at the last moment to tuck the ball into the nick, with it hardly touching their strings. Her heart sank when Jahangir blew past these players, and so did mine, but I knew Pa was right when he said Jahangir had it too, that Jahangir had all of it, and the difference was that Jahangir understood the power of the long game, where the ball is hunted, taken early, hit again and again to the back of the court. Khush sat cross-legged next to me, yawning, only half watching.

On her lap, she had Pa's letter sealed in its envelope,

which we would post on the way to Gujarati school. I knew she wanted to talk about opening it to see what Pa had written. We talked about that a lot, but we never did it. We made ourselves content with imagining what Pa might be saying to his friend. We imagined the description of details about us and our lives. The time we put on our training shirts and Pa took our photograph inside the court, all lined up against the front wall with the red service line at our backs, like film stars or suspects. The time we went to Wembley to see the playing fields where Jahangir trained with his cousin-coach Rahmat. The time one of us packed a rucksack with a block of cheese, a toothbrush, and clean underwear, and got as far as the enormous chestnut tree behind the flats before turning back because there were wasps. But we knew it would have nothing to do with us, the things Pa wrote in his letters. It would all be to do with the days in Mombasa when Pa and his brothers and his friend Bala were young and we didn't exist.

The TV went dark and then a new game started up. There was no sound for a few minutes. The picture was blurred, and when the sound came back it was loud and muffled. Khush passed me a sheet of kitchen towel. I wiped my chin. I felt suddenly sleepy and had an urge to lean my body into Khush's but she was concentrating on biting into her biscuit and orange. I was shivering. Khush hadn't gone out onto the landing at night since the time we had sat on the doorstep and I had asked her about it. I thought that maybe Khush had decided it wasn't Ma she had been talking to on the landing all this time. I thought that was the reason she had stopped. I'd also started to have episodes where I became convinced that Ma was returning. It always started with a cold feeling and if Khush was there I would always feel her watching me. The cold feeling came now.

I closed my eyes. The dampened sounds of the game on the TV got louder and the rain kept falling outside. I pushed a quarter of a biscuit into my mouth. It was soft from the orange. I tried to swallow and despite the softness the biscuit seemed to lodge in my throat. With my eyes closed, I saw the living room's purple swirled carpet with its deep pile and the blue curtains drawn back from the upstairs bedroom window, letting the daylight in. I saw everything as if I were Ma, returning and going about our house. I saw us: me and Khush in front of the TV, and Mona upstairs. But instead of thinking about going to Ma and pulling her wrists to make her come see what we were up to, I was thinking of what it would be like for her to come back to us here, to come back now. I didn't know if she had already been elsewhere too long.

I leaned forward and rested my cheek on my hand. Maybe, I thought, she would arrive eagerly only to find that things were too solid, and that we – our bodies – were too hard for her. I wondered would our touch bruise her. Would our talk hurt her ears. When we moved would we seem to fly past her, causing her to fall back. Would we seem different to her in ways so small she could never mention them for fear of our denials.

I looked at the sleeves of my sweatshirt. The grey fabric was stretched and there would soon be holes. I looked at Khush scratching her forearm, picking biscuit crumbs from the carpet. If Pa had not changed so completely, I thought, if he hadn't thrown himself so fully into our new routines, it would be different. Ma would stay and she would get used to us again.

The game on the TV was going on and on. There was a slight, shivery breeze and the sound of double doors opening and closing at the end of a corridor, the chlorine smell of pool water. And then everything was black and white and I knew I was dreaming because I saw Pa standing outside a squash court, occupied with his notebook, and Ma sitting on a nearby bench just looking at him. She didn't understand what she was seeing. I was on the court in Pa's ulster coat and in my hand was a racket with a new yellow grip. I had a vague feeling that there was something wrong with the grip, but I couldn't worry about that because I had to approach the glass wall and speak to Ma, explain to her what Pa was up to. If I didn't explain, then in a minute she would get up and leave because she would think there was no place for her in all this. But when I put my hand on the glass door, Pa gave me a dark, intimate glance that was both powerful and tender, and I knew there was something secret between the two of us that must be safeguarded. I looked at my grip, turned, and kept on with my drill.

'What is it?'

Khush's face was close to mine and her voice was strange and I realised she was on the verge of crying and it was because I was crying, not softly to myself, but with deep, swelling sobs, and my shoulders were shuddering and everything was like water. My hands and cheeks and mouth were wet. Khush held my shoulders and I just kept crying, with the feeling that it was coming from somewhere big and open inside me.

By the time Mona came downstairs, I was half dozing on the carpet in front of the video. Khush had put a blanket over me. On the TV, Jahangir was bringing his usual long game against Geoff Hunt, and though Khush had turned the volume down, I could hear their back-and-forth.

'We're not going to Gujarati class,' Khush said to Mona.

Mona was kicking her foot on the leg of the table behind us.

'Madhulaben will tell Pa,' she said.

She was right. Madhulaben would tell Pa and he wouldn't know what to say to her. I pulled myself up onto my elbow.

'It's okay,' I said. 'We can go.'

Khush looked at me closely. I tried to hold her gaze. My head was swimming.

'No,' she said.

The next thing, I was upstairs in my bunk with a hot water bottle and two blankets. I must have been in a fever for a week in all. I remember the blankets were heavy on me. They felt damp and warm. I remember the lamp being plugged in by my bed. I remember staring for hours at the crisscrossing metal frame of Mona's bed above me in the glow, and the slight depression in the frame when Mona was lying on it.

Pa never came into our bedroom, but he did then. Maybe it was only once. It was just me and him. He sat on the child's stool in front of the dressing table for a while, not saying anything, but as he was leaving he came by my bed and rested his hand lightly on my chest and then he tucked my blanket in such a way that for the whole night I didn't dare move in case I undid what he had done. My lamp glowed orange and I could hear my own heart beating softly.

Because Mona insisted on it, I stayed home while I recovered from my illness – but the whole time, Pa was getting me ready to return to Western Lane. He and I watched Bala's video late into the night, every night. I liked sitting up with Pa. Mona complained that I should be getting to bed early and Pa replied that I needed to keep my mind occupied. Eventually I returned to school but we continued staying up to watch the video and I found myself falling asleep in class, only jerking awake when I was called on by the teacher.

Maybe Mona finally decided that playing squash would be better for me than the late nights. One morning, Pa sat opposite me in the kitchen with his coat on, waiting for me to finish my cereal, and when I did, he said, 'I'll see you at Western Lane after your Gujarati class.'

Mona came in and she must have heard him. She got a bowl from the cupboard. She poured in her cereal without looking at me or Pa. Pa stood up and left for work.

We were the first to arrive, so we had to put the tables out. There were eighteen of us in all, between six and fifteen years old. We sat randomly, not organised by age or ability. We always drifted to the same haphazard positions we had taken from the beginning. Each student was supposed to pair with their neighbour and the older one would help the younger one to read, and then we would swap over. I was next to a boy named Hari who lived with his parents and grandmother in a room above a fruit and vegetable shop in Bury Park. Hari was seven and his Gujarati was better than mine. I let him read. It was warm in the hall and I was beginning to feel tired and wanted to go outside. I noticed a bruised, heavy feeling in my body. I could smell potatoes on Hari's breath and a mustiness coming up from his clothes.

Madhulaben watched us from the front of the class. Then she put her radio on, turned the heating up, and sat on the radiator at the far end of the hall, reading a Mills & Boon.

In the class, we tended to keep to ourselves. The other girls knew one another because they assembled to perform

Kathak dances and plays in the Queensway Hall. They didn't exclude us but we didn't know what to say to them and they didn't know what to say to us. I became aware of one of the older girls, Jinal, glancing up from her reading to stare at me and my sisters. After Ma died, we had been careful always to appear with our hair washed, our nails cut, our clothes clean. We did it instinctively, without conferring with one another, and we all sensed that this girl must now have found something amiss. We kept our heads down and tried not to think about it, but our three voices sounded loud and harsh, even with the tinny music from Madhulaben's radio and the buzz of everyone reading around us. I tried to read more quietly, which made Hari lean in close until his breath was on my cheek.

When Madhulaben rejoined the class her cheeks were flushed from sitting on the radiator. She smoothed the creases on the front of her kameez. She looked over our heads and waited for quiet so she could instruct us. She had us all copy a passage out of our text books. As usual, the passage she chose was hard to grasp, using grammar and vocabulary we didn't understand. I was content writing the passage. I didn't try to understand it. I just wrote it on a clean page, forming the letters as legibly as I could.

While Ma was still here, I had imagined that one day I would learn Madhulaben's passages by heart and then I would go home and recite them to Ma. I believed that Ma's thoughts came to her in language like this. And later when she was gone, I wished that I'd paid attention, that I'd learned, that I'd asked Madhulaben to tell us what it all meant.

After Madhulaben released us and we'd put the tables away and had our coats on, Jinal approached Mona in a deliberate way that suggested she had something to complain about.

'Hey, sorry about your mum,' she said.

It was obvious to us that this was not the main thing she wanted to discuss. We'd been in the same hall with Jinal a dozen times since Ma died, and she hadn't said anything about it. Jinal's father had died when Jinal was ten years old and we'd all put on our white tunics and gone to pay our respects the following day. Maybe she understood that it was odd, coming up to us now, after so long.

Mona said, 'Thanks,' and we would have walked on, but Jinal was still standing there. She had her coat on too, and she was partially blocking the doorway.

'How's your dad?' she asked. 'Because he came to fix our oven, and when he finished he left without saying anything and he hadn't touched his tea. Anyway my mum was wondering—'

'He's fine,' Mona said.

Jinal looked embarrassed.

'Okay, well,' she murmured. After a few seconds she made some excuse and went over to where her friends were waiting.

We had no idea what Jinal's mother was wondering and perhaps if Jinal had told us, it would have been nothing. But the way Jinal came at us, the way she stood, we knew it wasn't nothing, and we didn't want to know any more about it.

We hovered by the door until the girls had gone and then we got our bikes and cycled the long way to Western Lane.

The track outside the sports centre was wet, and none of us were looking forward to sprints. We were all thinking of Jinal's mother. We were imagining Pa standing against the wall, watching us train, and Jinal's mother emerging from the sports centre in her good sari to stand next to him, with two cups of tea.

We took our time in the changing room. I think I already knew, but when I went to the toilet I discovered I was bleeding. I wasn't frightened because Khush had explained it to me, but seeing the blood made me feel sick and upset.

Khush knocked on the cubicle door.

I came out and told her my period had started and she used the coins we were supposed to keep for emergencies to get a pad from the machine.

'Don't tell Mona,' I said.

Outside we stretched our calves and quads in silence. I put my hand on the wall for balance. Khush watched me.

'We don't have to run,' she said after a while.

'We do,' I said.

Mona looked at Khush, and at me. I dropped down to tighten the laces on my trainers. My face was burning and I was sure that Mona drew closer then, and we were back in the library, Mona whispering and whispering.

Three

When you are on the court, in the middle of a game, in a way you are alone. That is how it's supposed to be. You are supposed to find your own way out. You have to find the shots and make the space you need. You have to hold the T. No one can help you. No one can concentrate for you or fear losing on your behalf. But sometimes it seems the opposite is true. It seems that, on the court, you are not alone at all.

Mona had never been interested in playing. There was a sullenness about her, a tightness in her muscles, and a refusal of ease or rhythm in her movement. Khush hit well. She moved well. But she took a long time to recover from the physical crises that occurred naturally throughout play. I was the only one who was improving.

Twice, Pa sat down on the bench next to Khush while Mona and I were getting water. We heard him tell her that I needed meaningful competition if I was to advance. He said it in the same way that he would tell a stranger that he was expecting better weather.

Both times, Khush looked into the court with her hair sticking to her flushed cheeks. 'I'm doing my best,' she said.

Then one Monday, Pa cut our evening practice short and told me to wait at Western Lane by myself. He was going to drive my sisters home and after that he had a job in town. He told me to wait for Ged to come downstairs from the bar. He said I was going to play him. He said he would come to get me after, but he didn't seem in a hurry to go. He kept glancing towards the balcony. I heard Ged's mother upstairs, humming in a soft, scattered, slightly tuneless way as Pa slowly buttoned his coat.

I didn't know if I was supposed to ask Ged for a game or if Pa had already arranged it with him. I was at the water cooler filling a paper cone when Ged came downstairs.

He said, 'Hi,' and went to the message board, where he stood looking at the signing sheet for the league that someone was always trying to start up but was never able to really get going. There was a ballpoint pen Blu-Tacked upside down next to the paper.

On top of helping his mother with the glasses in the bar, it was Ged's job now to take care of the courts, which mainly meant keeping them clean and filling the water cooler. Depending on how things went, it might mean repainting the walls over the summer. The job had been

Ged's idea, and since the manager liked Ged's mother, he agreed to it. He paid Ged in cash. I sometimes thought Ged would have done it regardless, the way he looked so content and thoughtful once everything was clean. He was looking like that now, holding his rucksack and racket in one hand, studying the signing sheet. If the pen had dried out hanging upside down like that, I thought, I would offer him a pencil from my rucksack.

'It's spilling.'

The water from the cooler was overflowing my cone, onto the floor and the edge of my trainer. I lifted my thumb from the tap and stepped away.

Ged had paper towels in his bag. He laid his racket on the bench and came over.

'I can do it,' I said.

'It's okay.'

He was already crouched down, mopping the water pooling around the cooler.

'Are you going to join the league?' I asked.

Ged placed a final towel flat against the base of the cooler, then gathered the wet towels in one hand and stood up. I'd never seen Ged play against anyone else, and I had no idea if it was because he didn't have anyone or because he didn't want to. Ged opened the bin next to the cooler and put the towels inside.

'I don't know,' he said.

It seemed to me that he was going to walk away and so

I said, quickly, 'Do you want to play?' I blushed. 'I mean, with me.'

Ged looked at the top of the water cooler. He was thinking about how to put something.

'If you want to,' he said carefully. 'We don't have to.'

Pa had spoken to him.

'It's up to you,' I said.

He was quiet.

'Why d'you play?' he asked at last.

Ged had lost his stammer over the Christmas holidays, but it was still there underneath. It made him speak slowly, always. And with Ged, you would suddenly feel you were deep inside a conversation. I looked at the water in my cone. It didn't occur to Ged that it was a strange question to ask. It was something he wanted to know, and so he asked, and I wanted to attempt an answer. I thought of Pa, and of being on the court with Pa watching, and of the feeling when I forgot about Pa and I was just moving or striking the ball, and then the feeling when I wasn't playing. Ged stood waiting for me to work out what I thought. I thought: A game can seem endless. I said, 'I don't know.'

In the court with Ged, I had the feeling that we were making something, and it wasn't anything we could see or touch. I hit well. I saw the ball. It was as big as a tennis ball; I couldn't help but hit it well. I changed direction and lunged and there was a soft throbbing in my body from my toes to my fingertips. I moved easily and without effort. It was all Ged. He wasn't pushing me, exactly, but I felt that he was completely aware of me. He was also aware of the walls and the red out line and of the glass behind us and the corridor and the whole of the sports centre building: the empty swimming pool somewhere, the empty bar, the windows looking over distant fields. I felt his awareness of it all becoming mixed up with mine. Then I hit a volley drop that made Ged stop and look at me as if he did not know me, and that look made me stop too.

We sat on the bench outside the court. My T-shirt was damp and tight over my chest and I felt very conscious of it. I asked Ged if it was boring for him, playing against me.

'What do you think?' he said.

I looked at the racket he was holding in his hands.

'It's not boring,' he said.

We sat for a long time. We talked. I told Ged about a cave I had heard about. On the cave wall were paintings, mostly silhouettes of hands held against the wall, mostly left hands, hundreds and hundreds of them. It had been on the radio in our kitchen. From the size, experts had deduced the hands were those of ten-year-old boys, but I thought, How could they know if they were boys or girls. Ged asked if all the hand paintings had been made at the same time. How else? I thought. Then I thought maybe one child in every generation had been brought down into the deepest part of the cave to hold his or her palm to the wall. We pretended to listen to the footsteps above us and the muffled shouts of children diving into the swimming pool.

Ged began gathering his things. He got up from the bench.

'See you tomorrow,' he said.

I looked at him. I said, 'See you.'

He began to walk away.

He was going upstairs to the bar to help his mother. I didn't mean to speak or to make any sound at all but when I stood up, my racket banged on the bench and I heard myself calling out, 'Shall we play tomorrow?' When Ged turned to answer, he had the same look he'd had when I'd asked him the first time, and I understood the following day's game had also been arranged with Pa, but this time he said simply, 'I'd like that.'

A clean hit can stop time. Sometimes it can feel like the only peace there is.

Ged and I played three times that winter and more or less every day of spring. My thoughts became very clear in those months. I got up early in the mornings, not to be alone, but because the whole night I had been waiting for the day to begin.

At Western Lane, when the Vauxhall men were on the court and all the doors were open, and the trees were white with blossoms outside, I stood very still next to Ged and he was still too. Maybe it only happened once but I remember our standing like this as if it had occurred at intervals throughout my childhood. I stopped thinking of Ma. The world seemed big and luminous with some secret that would soon be known to me.

One Sunday, Ged and I were warming up and Pa was watching us. The outside doors opened and two Pakistani men about Pa's age came in, dressed in white T-shirts and white shorts. I knew the men by sight. They were nice, steady players and Pa had become friendly with them. One carried a bulky sports bag with Dunlop printed across it. The shaft of a white racket stuck out from inside the bag.

This man's name was Maqsud. When Maqsud first came to Western Lane, he and Pa had been wary of one another. It was Maqsud who had made the first move. In the bar, Maqsud had offered Pa a drink and before he accepted, Pa had talked a little. It seemed to be about nothing, but somehow, in this nothing, Pa made it known to Maqsud that we (he gestured with his hand to indicate that he meant himself and us) were Jains. At home, Mona tried to make an argument of it. 'If we are all brothers, why does it matter that we are Jains?' she demanded. 'It matters,' Pa said, and went back to his paperwork.

Now, Maqsud greeted Pa while his friend proceeded to the next court. Ged and I hit volleys.

'That's the young one?' we heard Maqsud ask Pa. He had a kind, gravelly voice.

Ged and I completed our warm-up and began a game,

aware of Maqsud watching us. We played fast and placed the ball well. I was retrieving the ball from a corner when Maqsud made a beckoning motion with his hand, calling me over, and so I let the ball drop and nudged it with my racket towards Ged before approaching the back wall.

'There is a tournament in the winter,' Maqsud said. His voice through the glass was low and confiding, but somehow projected so that it included Ged. 'Durham and Cleveland. You should enter, both of you.'

We passed Durham whenever we went to Edinburgh. It was a long drive. There was a castle that was always lit orange at night. I wanted Maqsud to say something more. It was hypnotising, the way his voice was both hard and soft. Pa went to the bench to look at his notebook and now Maqsud spoke only to me.

'Your father believes in you,' he said. 'Because inside that court you are as tough as a boy. Do you know that?'

I looked down at my racket and tremblingly adjusted my strings. I heard Ged's racket knock the wall and I jumped because I felt as if he was knocking on something right in front of me. I felt very close to Ged, and to Pa, and to this man. Maqsud was waiting for me to speak. I brushed my hand over the face of my racket, trying to keep my fingers still.

'Not any boy,' I heard myself say.

There was silence and then Maqsud was laughing. I glanced up and so did Pa. I could see he was surprised and pleased.

'Durham and Cleveland,' Maqsud said, and joined his friend next door.

From that day on, Ged and I listened out for Maqsud's voice in the corridors whenever we were training. The words Durham and Cleveland began to accumulate meaning for us. We imagined a dark landscape covered in snow, glass courts glittering in the winter sun. Or we imagined somewhere entirely ordinary, grey, concrete.

'Durham and Cleveland,' one of us would say suddenly for no reason, and we'd sit for a while.

I got up earlier and earlier in the mornings. On weekends and holidays, when the sky was still black outside, I laid out eight slices of bread on the kitchen table and made sandwiches that I pressed into a lunch box. Then I cycled to Western Lane in the dark. By the time I was locking my bike, the sky was lighter but there was no colour in the grass or the trees. I did timed sprints on the running track outside until the sports centre opened and I could go in and practise on one of the courts. You couldn't use the courts until 7.30 a.m. so if I was early I sat on a bench and waited. The manager stood in the corridor watching me practise one morning, and later he found me and told me that as long as a court was free, I could use it, it didn't matter what time it was.

Pa and Maqsud talked about Durham and Cleveland, and then Pa talked to me. He said Ged's mother had agreed to let Ged compete. He said the tournament would be good for me, but there was a fee and the family would have to contribute towards the petrol for the drive and towards accommodation if one of us got through the first day. I didn't know if he meant that I could go or not.

'We don't have the money?' I said.

'It's not so much,' Pa said.

I looked at his hands turning the steering wheel. I felt that he was waiting for me to speak.

He glanced at me and back at the road.

'It's up to you,' he said.

I tried to read his face.

'I want to go,' I said.

Pa smiled. 'That's what I thought,' he said.

Sometimes, when I was at Western Lane by myself, all I did was hit drives to the back of the court. I was happy whatever I was doing. My forehand was already strong and so I focused on my backhand. At first I had to concentrate on keeping my distance from the ball, but in a few days I was hitting well without having to think about it. I hesitated then. I didn't know how long I could hold on to what I had learned by myself or even whether I had learned something useful.

Pa often came late in the morning and stayed much of the day. If he had work, he started me off with drills and returned when he could. He went up to the balcony often, and I would hear him talking with Ged's mother if she came out from the bar to say hi.

Pa made a column for Ged in his notebook. When Ged and I practised drills in the evening, Pa directed us. When we played a game, sometimes Pa watched us. Sometimes, he and Ged's mother stood under the security light on the other side of the double doors that led to the car park, sharing a cigarette. We kept playing when they went outside. If my gaze strayed to the doors, Ged would stop and look at me. 'Ready?' he'd say quietly, as if he was bringing me back from somewhere, and we would continue playing.

Four

The Australian Geoff Hunt believed that the Pakistani players he came up against on the squash court hunted him as a pack. During tournaments, rather than discussing how they would win the event, these players would get together and discuss how they would beat Hunt, because once Hunt was beaten, one of them was sure to bring the trophy home.

I used to imagine Hiddy Jahan and Gogi Alauddin and Qamar Zaman and Mohibullah Khan all dressed in their winter coats, standing over a table in a darkened hotel room late into the night, solemnly and vigorously debating each player's tactics against this one man. I imagined a hearth in which a few flames flickered, causing shadows to lengthen on the hotel room walls, and as the conference went on, the flames grew and the men's voices deepened.

After Maqsud came into our lives, we often stood in the court, Maqsud, Pa, Ged and I, and went over our training programme for the tournament in Durham, and I would think of those winter conferences. Pa would be in his suit, while Maqsud, Ged and I would be in our training clothes with our rackets and rucksacks at our feet. We discussed our strengths and weaknesses and how we might use or overcome them. I knew how to move on the court, and sometimes I hit beautiful, aggressive shots, but I was inconsistent. Ged had court sense. He knew where he was and where his opponent was and he knew where to place the ball. In this way, he was an attacking player, but sometimes, when he had done the work, when he had set himself up to win, his mind wandered. During our conferences, Pa and Maqsud listened as carefully to what Ged and I had to say as they did to each other. Occasionally Maqsud interjected with a story. One of his favourite subjects was Gogi Alauddin. Gogi came from a poor family. When he was young, two businessmen saw him play and they helped him by giving him rackets and milk. Gogi became very motivated. There were not many players in Lahore, where Gogi lived, and sometimes he took on two men at once in order to give himself competition. Gogi was never number one but he was one of the greats, Maqsud said.

Mona and Khush began watching me closely. They were aware that something was happening at Western Lane, and that they were not part of it. I knew Mona would tell me what she thought about it, and she did. She said that Pa allowed me to play Ged because no one would find out what went on in the sports centre. She meant no one from our family, no one from Gujarati school, no one Pa visited.

No one, she said, would know that a white boy and I were playing sports together. No one would know that we were manoeuvring around one another, sweating, wiping our palms along the same smudged patch of wall, first him, then me.

'Pa didn't allow it,' I said. 'He arranged it. And he told Bala.'

The three of us were in the fort behind the house. We had our tennis rackets but had lost the ball so we were sitting until we decided on something else to do.

'He didn't tell Bala,' Mona said.

She kept bouncing the rim of her racket head on the concrete floor.

'Bala doesn't count,' she added after a while.

I looked at Khush.

'Pa talks to Ged's mother sometimes,' I said.

I wasn't addressing Mona, but Mona stood up and walked out of the fort. Khush and I watched her for a minute and then collected our coats and rackets and followed.

'He doesn't,' Mona said when we caught her up.

'He does.'

My sisters already knew Pa smoked outside with Ged's mother, and I felt bad mentioning it, because it was private. It had nothing to do with us.

Mona murmured something about Aunt Ranjan.

Jinal, the girl from Gujarati class, had eventually delivered her mother's message. Her mother was inviting all of us to her house for dinner. Jinal hadn't wanted to ask us, any more than we had wanted to be asked. Mona had told her we would have to check with Pa, but when she told Pa about the invitation, she added, 'We already said no.' Pa asked if we had thanked her and Mona said we had, and that was that, as far as Pa was concerned. Aunt Ranjan found out about the invitation from Jinal's Kathak teacher, who was friends with Jinal's mother. Aunt Ranjan phoned Pa but Pa wasn't home and so she asked Mona what was going on. 'Nothing is going on, Auntie,' Mona replied. 'Pa said we couldn't go.' Aunt Ranjan must have been satisfied with this because she put Uncle Pavan on. We were all wondering now what Aunt Ranjan would say about Pa sharing cigarettes with Ged's mother.

'It's nothing,' Mona said. 'It's just talking.'

But there was something about the way Pa talked to Ged's mother. He told her what he thought about things, and asked her what she thought. We had never heard him talk this way with Ma or our aunties or any of the women we knew.

The start of that summer was as sunny and blue-skied as any we remembered. At Western Lane, when Pa came in from smoking outside with Ged's mother, we would not have been surprised had they trod sand or salt water into the corridor. Ged's mother wore yellow sandals and her toenails were painted pink. She was nice. She always said hello and remembered things you had said to her. It was better when my sisters weren't there at these times, because when they were present, Mona's disapproval hung over everything.

Since she couldn't talk to Pa about Ged's mother, Mona talked about the cigarettes, and, without saying so, she was talking about money. Pa smoked Camels, which he bought one packet at a time.

'Do you know how many packets it is now, Pa?' she'd say.

Pa would glance up from his paper.

'You will tell me.'

And Mona, who had been ready to exclaim that it was four packets a week, would change the subject. Abbreviated exchanges like this took place in our kitchen more or less daily that summer.

Mona planned the week's meals meticulously but Pa was doing less work, telling people he was too busy or else simply missing appointments by not turning up, and there was never any money left over. Though we weren't hungry, the food we had was not enough to sustain me on the court. I became nauseous doing sprints. My muscles tired easily.

One day, I played through a sprain in my right ankle. Pa didn't notice until the following morning because after the initial jolt I had played on and he had gone out to smoke. Ged noticed. Since I didn't mention it, he didn't either, but he played the ball to my racket so that I wouldn't have to run or land heavily on my backhand. He took a long time to serve and he adjusted the strings on his racket between rallies. It made my head buzz, the way he checked where I was, the way he placed the ball lightly.

At home, when the others were sleeping, I went downstairs and prepared a turmeric paste which I smoothed over the tender part of my foot. I covered it with an old sports sock. I removed it in the bath in the morning. The sock was yellow inside and full of the turmeric that had come away from my foot in dried, powdery lumps. There wasn't much swelling but it hurt when I put my weight on the foot, which made me limp a little. When Pa saw me limp he had me sit with my leg up on a chair and got peas out of the freezer to ice the foot. He made me a hot water bottle. Then he sat with me and said I should have told him. After twenty minutes, he put the peas back in and we waited for them to freeze again. Mona said we couldn't eat them now because they'd been thawed and refrozen. She wrote 'Foot' on a white label, which she stuck to the packet of peas so that we wouldn't eat them later by accident. I was back on the court after a couple of days.

The next time I sprained my ankle, the pain was worse from the beginning and it took a long time to heal. Pa and I had been on the court for an hour when it happened. I'd been feeling sluggish and I wasn't seeing the ball. Pa said he knew I was tired, but sometimes you have to play through the tiredness. He said keep your eye on the ball. But I couldn't. I had to pivot sharply and run to get to every ball and in the end my ankle just gave way. I felt the pain like a cold shock inside my head. Everything went black and I was on the floor. I remember Pa helping me off the court, though I thought I could still walk. He was in his training clothes, white trousers and white T-shirt, and I remember thinking how I had disappointed him, and how nice he looked, and I remember leaning heavily on his arm.

Pa gave me painkillers and this time he made the turmeric paste. He wrapped my ankle and had me rest and ice it. Mona stood at the sink watching us with her arms folded, and in the evening when Pa was upstairs bathing, she filled a plastic basin with warm water and lowered it to the floor in front of me. Some of the water spilled and my bandage got wet.

I said, 'Pa will do it.'

'Pa's tired,' she said.

She washed the turmeric from my foot and made a new paste, which she applied neatly, exactly where it was swelling. She was really gentle with it. She had the concentrating expression that Ma had when she was sifting flour or cleaning a cut. I said thank you, and she nodded. Her glance flickered to her reflection in the glass in the door behind me.

Pa came down. When he saw what Mona had done he looked at her briefly and sat at the table to write his letters.

Sometimes it hurt even when I had my leg up, but it was a dull hurt and I could usually make it go away by turning my foot one way or the other. I stayed off school until the swelling had gone down and I could put my trainers on. I told Pa I could walk, but he drove us. Pa went to work some of the time and my sisters and I went to school, and no one went to the sports centre.

Three weeks passed and I began dreaming of Western Lane. I saw the white walls and the blossoms outside. At night I got out of bed and went over to the windows where there was a bit of light coming through the curtains. I sat on the floor with my racket, my back against the radiator. It was silent now because it was no longer on. I fixed a new grip onto my racket inexpertly, then peeled the tape off and fixed it again. Sometimes I did my exercises, standing on one foot in the half light, lowering my body carefully and straightening again. I ignored Mona when she told me to go back to bed, and after a while she just lay on her side and watched me.

During those weeks away from Western Lane, Pa went to bed early, not emerging from his room until after we'd left for school, and he was tired every day. As far as we could tell, he was still working, but he was letting Mona take care of everything at home. The only thing he did himself was write the cheque for my place in the tournament, but even this he allowed Mona to address and post.

Mona sat in front of the dressing table mirror for long stretches of time. She developed a placid expression, which made her look older. When at last we returned to Western

Lane, she seemed to commit herself to a new relationship with Pa and us. She began to manage everything in the house, but she sought Pa's opinions on things and listened to what he said. She served me extra dal and rice and took less for herself. She asked me if I had changed out of my damp clothes after training, and she asked Khush about her homework. She was attentive to us, even kind. Sometimes we could feel the strain in her, the mental and physical burden of being something she was not.

We were all at Western Lane when Maqsud's nephew turned up. Shaan was sixteen. He was good looking. Maqsud told us that his nephew was visiting for the afternoon, that he lived in Coventry with his grandparents, and that he was going to compete alongside me and Ged in the tournament in January. While we performed drills, Shaan stood in the corridor with Maqsud, discussing the match going on in the other court. We could see that Maqsud was very interested in what Shaan had to say.

We had been playing for twenty minutes when I noticed that Shaan kept glancing into our court. Mona noticed too. She looked like a different player suddenly. Her racket was up and she was stepping into her swing. She was hitting quite well. I thought she looked angry but then I thought it was something else. I watched her, mesmerised by the change in her, until, in the middle of a drill, she turned, let her racket arm fall, and walked to the back of the court, where she opened the door calmly and stepped out. She stood next to Pa and spoke to him in a low voice. When Khush and I swung round and stared at her, she looked at the wall behind us and re-tied her ponytail with jerky movements. Her eyes were bright and her face was flushed.

All the way home, Mona talked about Durham and Cleveland.

She continued the next day, and the next. The tournament was months away, but soon it became a habit for us to discuss the logistical arrangements again and again. Pa, Ged and I were going to drive up with Maqsud and collect his nephew on the way. If any one of us got through to the second day, we would stay the night in Newcastle with Maqsud's cousin who owned a restaurant. That way we wouldn't have to pay for a hotel. Mona talked about the food we would need, and whether Maqsud's cousin was going to feed us or whether we'd have to pack food for two days.

At Western Lane, Mona played a little but more often she went off to find Maqsud. It was after one of her conversations with Maqsud that Mona announced she and Khush were going to come with us to Durham and Cleveland. They weren't going to play. They were coming to support me. She said Maqsud thought it was a good idea. Pa said fine and turned up the volume on his radio.

Mona watched him and it slowly dawned on her that he already knew all about it, that maybe it had even been his idea.

She crossed to the sink. She ran the hot water tap until it was steaming and began washing up. Then suddenly she stopped. She turned around and said, 'I've taken a job.'

Pa switched his radio off then.

Mona dried her hands carefully, sat down opposite him and said she was going to start helping out at one of the hair salons on Leagrave Road. She would be washing hair, sweeping floors, cleaning windows, or whatever needed doing. Under Pa's gaze, she lowered hers and said she needed something to occupy her. She didn't mention what she would be earning, or anything to do with money. There was a silence, and then Pa said he would talk to the manager of the salon. Mona looked at him curiously. She asked why, and he said he wanted to know who she would be working for. Something about this pleased Mona, I think. She made Pa promise that if he had to call the manager then he would do so the following day and he would not say anything to embarrass her. Pa kept his word, and he must have been satisfied because from then on, every Thursday evening and Saturday morning, Mona left Khush with lists of chores and went out to work.

A few times, Mona had to look after the tills at the hair salon because two of the staff kept getting sick. She talked to the manager about his finances. Because he saw she was honest and clever with money, the manager gave her the bookkeeping to do, and he told the owners of the three-storey pet shop and the garden centre across the road. Before long, Mona was bringing home the paperwork from all these places and working on it at night.

One evening, she started trying to talk to Pa about my training.

'I read that she shouldn't lift weights too close to the event,' she said. It was one of those weeks when she had headaches and her mood wouldn't settle. Pa just looked at her, because I wasn't lifting weights at all.

She looked back at him, and then she said casually that maybe we would go and get me a new racket.

I stared at her, and at the glass of chaas in front of me. Pa mixed his dal into his rice. He glanced at me.

'Is that what you want?' he asked.

I concentrated on my glass and thought of Maqsud's white Dunlop racket with its big teardrop head. Pa held his spoonful of rice in mid-air, and I heard myself say, 'Yes.'

I held my breath. Mona made a small noise as if to encourage Pa to say something.

'Very well,' Pa said.

Mona waited, but there was no more.

She said she would pay for the racket out of her wages.

'We have to get it soon,' she said. 'She has to get used to it before the tournament.'

Pa finished his rice, put his plate in the sink and went into the living room.

Mona followed him with her eyes, and then looked at me.

'I'd really like a racket,' I said.

In the winter, Pa and I had had a long discussion about the rackets used by the Vauxhall men, a few of which were wooden, though most were aluminium and fibreglass. We had discussed the pros and cons of each until Pa closed his notebook and said that Jahangir Khan played with wooden rackets, the same as us. But ever since Maqsud had first talked to us, I had dreamed of a Dunlop like his. Open throat, that was what the teardrop shape was called.

My sisters and I went on the train to London.

Pa said it would be better to spend the money on the racket than on a ticket for him. He dropped us at the station and told us he was going to go to work.

He didn't say anything in advance about which racket I should get, and I didn't ask him. I asked Maqsud. Maqsud said I would know once I had the racket in my hand.

It was Maqsud who had told Mona where we should go. The shop was on a side street with garbage bags on the pavement. It didn't look like much from the outside. But inside, the shop was like nothing I had ever seen. It was brightly lit, with rackets covering every wall. They were mostly tennis rackets but the whole of one wall was for squash. There must have been a thousand squash rackets.

Mona told the manager in the shop how much she could afford and he thought about it for a while. Then he brought out five rackets for me, and none of them were wooden. If I asked him to bring me a wooden racket he would, I thought. I picked up the rackets he had chosen, one at a time.

'You can swing,' the manager said. 'If you like, you can go outside. Hit a ball against the wall.'

'It's okay,' I said.

There was one racket.

It was all silver. It wasn't the same as Maqsud's but it had the teardrop head, and Maqsud was right. I knew as soon as I held it.

'That's a very good one for the price,' the manager said.

When he handed me the bag with my new racket inside, I was so happy I didn't know what to do. The manager looked like he was going to say something but he just cleared his throat and went back to his till.

Outside the shop, Mona said, 'Let's get milkshakes.'

We sat on a sunny bench at the edge of a park, my new silver racket on my knees.

The milkshakes were thick, with big scoops of ice cream. We swapped so we could try all the flavours.

'This is great,' Khush said.

It was. The sky was blue and the buildings around the park were white and tall and we kept sitting there in the sun, swapping milkshakes.

Mona had kept a bit of money back, so we went into a department store and the assistants on the make-up counter persuaded Khush to get her eyes made up. She sat on a high stool, and we all watched. Then Mona sat for the assistant, and she looked nice made up, but not like Khush. My sisters bought lipsticks. I said I didn't want anything. I said Mona had already bought me my racket, but Mona chose a colour for me and tried it on my lips, and Khush said it looked pretty and we should get it. People kept looking at us, mostly at Khush, who sat on the edge of her seat in her grey leggings and sweatshirt, her eyes so lovely you could cry just looking at her.

We were still excited from our outing when we arrived home. Instead of going inside, I sat on the doorstep with my racket. Khush came back out and sat with me.

'You okay?' she asked.

I nodded. We watched the light come out of the sky slowly and the stars start to appear. I thought that if Fourth Avenue came around the garages now, we wouldn't care, we would still sit there watching the sky because there was nothing he could do to us.

Pa had made rice and dal. We could smell the starch and spices from the doorstep. It reminded us that we were hungry. In the kitchen, the radio was on and Pa was serving. He passed us the plates he was holding and asked us how our day had been. I leaned my racket, still in its bag, against my leg while we ate. Pa avoided looking at us. He didn't mention the make-up and it was only after we had finished eating and Mona had gathered our plates and she and Khush were busying themselves with cleaning that Pa mentioned my racket. I took it out of the bag and unzipped it from its cover before giving it to him. My sisters paused in their work to watch.

Holding the racket so that its face was open, Pa adjusted his grip. He frowned slightly, adjusted again. The radio buzzed on, and slowly we understood that we had made a terrible mistake in going to London, in spending Mona's money.

Pa ran a thumb around the silver frame. After a long time, he put my racket on the table between us.

'It is very nice,' he said. 'You did well.'

He said this, but with his eyes and his body – his shoulders, his throat, the white bones visible under his skin – he was telling us that in one day we had exposed him, left him behind, left him wide open to whatever was coming for him.

He rose and put a hand on Mona's shoulder before going upstairs.

We switched the radio off and finished clearing up. We stood by the kitchen door looking out into the unlit hallway.

'What are we going to do?' I whispered.

Khush picked up my racket from the table and handed it to me.

'Nothing,' she said. 'We're going to go to bed.'

Five

In 1983, the Egyptian Gamal Awad, known as the Grasshopper, was defeated by Jahangir Khan in the longest match in the game's history. Two hours and forty-six minutes in a Perspex court on the stage of the Chichester Festival Theatre. Gamal Awad was known for his speed and acrobatics. In the game against Jahangir Khan, he dived for the ball and recovered position again and again in a way that seemed impossible to those watching. But then Gamal Awad tried to slow the game down, and Jahangir did the same. Each man bet on the other making mistakes, which neither did, and long periods of the match became quite boring. Gamal Awad had intended to test Jahangir Khan's endurance, and Jahangir Khan intended to make sure no one went away with the impression that he could be beaten in a long match. In the end Jahangir was tired, but the Grasshopper was exhausted. Legend had it that the Grasshopper was never the same after that day. In 1987, he received a ban when he threw his racket at a referee, and soon after, he retired from the game.

From the back of Maqsud's dusty, hot Peugeot, we listened to Maqsud's stories and were spellbound. All the windows were open. Maqsud didn't shout, but it seemed to us that his voice was everywhere. He had removed the shelf over the boot so that Khush and I could sit in there with our legs outstretched. Ged, his mother, Mona and Maqsud's nephew Shaan were in the back seat and Pa was in the passenger seat. We were on our way to a funfair in Leicester.

It had been Shaan's idea but it was Mona who had persuaded Pa.

'We need to do something,' she had said to Pa. 'We need something to look forward to.'

Pa had put his pen on the table and rubbed his shoulder.

'You go,' he said. 'But it's expensive.'

'It's free.'

'When you get there it will be expensive.'

'You have to come. There's no point otherwise.'

She turned away from him to the cooker and began stirring sugar into the milk she was warming.

'Ged's coming,' she murmured, 'and so's his mother.'

Pa didn't agree to it, but he didn't make any more objections.

We had come off the motorway in Coventry and stopped at a newsagent shop to collect Shaan, who came out of the shop as soon as we parked, squeezed in next to Mona, and put his rucksack on his knees before passing around sweets made of condensed milk and sugar and pistachios, sent by his grandmother.

'Alright,' he'd said to all of us at once.

He smelled strongly of soap. His voice hadn't completely filled out yet, but you could tell that one day it would be like Maqsud's voice. The white shirt he was wearing was plain, like a work shirt, but on him it was almost beautiful.

Khush nudged my feet with hers. The back of Mona's neck and her upper arms were a blotchy pink and she was leaning forward and talking quietly to Maqsud, as if she was very interested in having a conversation with him.

'Maybe it wasn't because of Jahangir that the Grasshopper threw that racket. I mean, it was years later, wasn't it? Maybe it was in his nature all along.' Her voice was high and slightly breathless.

'Maybe,' Maqsud said. 'We don't know.'

I was thinking it seemed like bad luck that this man, whose play Maqsud said was miraculous, was being remembered for throwing his racket, when Maqsud said softly, 'But Gamal Awad is not just one thing.'

Mona half turned and passed the sweets back to us, avoiding meeting our eyes. Her arm brushed Shaan's beautiful white shirt.

Deep down, the funfair was a sad place. You couldn't hear yourself think. Everything was too bright and too big. The floor was covered in sawdust and underneath it, dirt. On the other side of the Round Up there was a wire fence around a patch of muddy grass with a few bits of hay, and inside the fence was the saddest saddest horse you ever saw. Chestnut brown with white socks, covered in flies, its nose more or less touching the ground because its own head was too much for its neck to bear. It wasn't just sad: there was something mean in it that wasn't its fault. When I whispered to it, *hello horse*, it slowly turned its whole body away.

But then there were the eight of us. Though we had agreed we would split up and all meet at 7.00 p.m. in front of the Ferris wheel, for a long time we just stayed together, talking excitedly, pointing at the pink and white striped huts of the coconut shy and duck shooting stall, breathing in the air that was filled with the smell of caramelised sugar and things burning. Maqsud and Shaan came back from somewhere before we knew they'd gone, each holding four cones of whipped vanilla ice cream.

Even when we separated, first the children all in one group and the adults in another, then Mona and Shaan disappearing so it was just me and Khush and Ged, we were aware of ourselves dispersed throughout the fair, and when one group glimpsed another we lit up and lingered for as long as it took to tell about what we'd seen. The boys running the rides swore and shouted and sometimes climbed on the outside of a painted car or aeroplane that was swinging up into the air, and held on for their lives. Here and there were circus things that you didn't have to pay to look at, such as children dressed in yellow clothes who kept making and remaking a human pyramid, a sad-happy juggler on a unicycle, a beautiful couple on a tightrope.

Near the toilets, Khush, Ged and I watched Mona and Shaan pouring whisky into two bottles of Coke, and later Mona bought Cokes for us, and then shandies for Pa and Ged's mother and Maqsud, but she made sure she went with Pa to buy the drinks so that no one knew it was her money that paid for them.

When the five of us, my sisters and Shaan and Ged and I, got into the car of the Twister, the sun was almost above us and we could barely sit on the metal seat, it was so hot. We couldn't touch the metal anywhere. We raised our arms up in the air. My shoulders touched Ged's on one side, Khush's on the other, and we soared and shouted as the car flew up almost vertically on the rails and plummeted down. From the highest point we spotted the top of Maqsud's head and then Pa and Ged's mother smoking near the coconut shy and we shouted and shouted until they all looked up. Our legs shook when we put our feet back on the ground. Ged's hand shot out to steady me when I swayed. I stood there dizzily staring at the mud, my heart thumping. I felt something powerful move from me to Ged and then he let go but it didn't seem to matter because the thing was still there.

We needed more sugar. More Coke, more ice cream, candy floss spinning in a hopper, then dissolving in our open mouths. Mona was generous and she didn't wait for us to ask. It was as if she wanted to spend all the money she had, and that was alright with us. Pa let me taste one of his shandies. I took a big swig. It was cold and then warm in my stomach. Pa smiled at me and I looked over at Ged and then at the spinning Round Up, whose outline was suddenly perfectly sharp and clear in front of us.

Shaan had friends at the funfair. His friends were all sixteen or seventeen. They looked older. A few of them had skateboards, and one of those was a girl. You weren't supposed to bring bikes in but no one said anything about skateboards. The girl with the skateboard had a tiny diamond nose stud and dark hair that came down to her waist. Her skateboard had 7 SECONDS sprayed across it in black paint. Shaan introduced Mona to her, and it was obvious something was up because Shaan kept checking for the skateboard girl's reaction. Later, it looked like Shaan and the girl were arguing. Or rather, they were both leaning against a wall and Shaan was smoking and saying things offhandedly as if he was bored but you could see he wasn't bored. The girl was just looking the other way. Her diamond stud caught the light when she looked down to flick ash off her cigarette. Shaan stopped talking and she pushed off from the wall, picked up her skateboard, and strode towards the rest of her group. She didn't say a word to Shaan. Shaan watched her. He looked miserable, but not as miserable as Mona. She was by herself near the toilets. Her eyes had been fixed on Shaan but now they were lowered, and there was something odd about her mouth.

Khush and I went over to Mona, and the three of us began to walk through the fair. We passed the shooting stalls and the human pyramid and the Ferris wheel. Maybe we would have left the fair but there was nowhere to go and so we kept walking round. Mona's mouth began to look normal again. She put her hands in her skirt pockets. People smiled at us with shining eyes. On the other side of the Round Up, the chestnut horse behind the wire lifted its head to watch us, then dropped it again.

Underneath the pity and the sadness I felt for Mona there was the invisible thing that was happening between me and Ged. It made my heart stand up. Sit down, I whispered to it as we walked, but it didn't want to. Khush slowed to look at the human pyramid.

We felt the brittleness return to Mona's body.

Mona was digging into something in her head and she wanted to draw us into whatever it was.

She looked at the space in front of her.

'If Ma wasn't dead,' she said dully, 'Ged and his mother wouldn't be here.'

Then she turned her head to address me.

'They're only here because Ma is dead. Do you understand?'

I kept walking alongside her. She asked me again if I had understood. She wanted an answer.

But it wasn't me who answered.

Suddenly, Mona and I felt a wave of something hot and white come at us. Maybe Mona could have swung around but it was too late because Khush was flying at her. Khush, who was so slight, was knocking Mona to the ground.

Mona must have been off balance because there was no resistance in her until she was in the mud and then she was scrapping. I noticed the flies buzzing around the horse, its neck suddenly strong as it raised its head right up and watched us. I saw everything about that horse. The animal strength in its muscles, the hard itch in its hoof, the stench in its mouth, and I don't know how because I was down there too, with my sisters. Everything was bones and hooves and hot breath. I tasted blood, hot and sweet.

Then someone's hands were on my shoulders, lifting me up.

It was Maqsud. The smell of sweat was so sharp on him, I thought it was me, or the horse. I saw that Ged had Khush and at the same time he was bending to help Mona get up.

Maqsud addressed me, telling me carefully that everything was going to be alright. And with one hand flat across Khush's breastbone, holding her apart from Mona, Ged was watching me, and his face told me the same thing: everything was going to be alright. What they were really saying was that I should stay where I was. They were telling me to be still.

Pa and Ged's mother saw the mud on our legs, and the grazes, and the blood. Ged's mother looked at Ged. Pa touched our shoulders and necks and swallowed his drink. Maqsud bought more drinks and suddenly, inexplicably, the hurt feelings in us seemed like nothing as we all stood in a row against the side of the duck shooting stall and watched the sun set. Then we watched the moon. It was barely visible against the light sky. I stood next to Ged and I kept saying to myself, Everything is going to be alright.

Mona stopped going to work. She stopped going anywhere except school and Western Lane, and to the cash and carry when Pa agreed to take us, or else to the VG store. The manager of the hair salon phoned up and Mona said she had too much homework and couldn't come any more, and would he let the others know please. But she continued to take care of the house.

Khush and I sat in the fort behind the house and went over what had happened at the funfair. Khush said that Mona liked Shaan, but even before 7 Seconds had turned up with her skateboard, Mona wasn't going to do anything about it. Mona couldn't bear the thought of Aunt Ranjan or anyone else calling Pa to complain that his daughter was going around with a Pakistani boy, and what about the shame on Ma, who was gone? While Ma was alive, whenever we did something we weren't supposed to, our relatives would bring Ma's feelings into it, as if she was easy to hurt. But she wasn't. It didn't matter now. Now she was gone, our capacity to hurt her seemed infinite.

Mona did have homework, and so did Khush. They came to Western Lane for only an hour a day and, soon, only on Saturdays. It was their decision and Pa did not question it. I no longer practised with them at all. Once, Maqsud brought his cousin's daughter for me to play but she didn't like my hitting hard and by the time I realised this, it was too late, and after that it was just me and Pa and Ged.

Pa and I returned home from Western Lane late in the evenings, and it would seem to me that a long time had passed since I'd seen my sisters. I'd open the fridge to get milk or head straight out into the garden to go up and down the path on my skates and replay the week's games inside my head. Sometimes, skating up the path, I would think of Ged, of his steadying me when I came off the Twister, or his placing the ball when I was hurt, and I would let myself remember, and then I would no longer be in the garden. When, finally, I came in, Pa would look up from his papers and he would just stare as if he was startled.

'It's Ma,' Khush would tell me later. 'You look like Ma.'

If we arrived at home to find that Mona hadn't cooked, Pa would wait for me to come in and he'd send me and Khush to the VG store. We'd come home with tins of baked beans and mini frozen pizzas, which would make Mona angry with the three of us. What visitors we had were very interested in what we ate every day and this, too, made Mona angry. Her moods did not seem to trouble Pa. He didn't seem to notice.

One evening, I became nauseous on the court and Pa, who was on the balcony with Ged's mother, came down and told me I needed to eat something. I didn't know what to say to him. The following day, Ged's mother came to our house. She stood on the doorstep and said she had brought us a dish of lasagne because she'd made extra, but she wasn't going to stay.

Pa said, 'Mona was just making tea.'

She came in.

'There's no meat in it,' she explained to Mona.

Mona told me to make the tea and then she put on her coat and went out.

Ged's mother wasn't sure what to do, but since Pa had invited her, she put the lasagne dish on the empty worktop and sat down at the kitchen table, and I made the tea. We all thought Mona wasn't going to come back, but she did. She had with her a whole shop-bought madeira cake, which she opened and sliced up and dropped in the middle of the table. We drank our tea and ate the cake. Then Pa and Ged's mother stood outside in the garden.

They were still outside when the doorbell rang a second time.

It was Susilaben, Jinal's mother. She came into the kitchen and saw the teacups and cake crumbs and Pa and Ged's mother smoking in the garden. Khush went to get Pa.

Susilaben smiled nervously at me and Mona.

'You're cooking for your father?' she asked Mona after a while.

'Pa can cook,' Mona said. 'He can look after himself.'

Susilaben blinked and looked around our kitchen until Pa came in with Ged's mother.

'This is Linda,' Pa said. 'Susila.'

The two women greeted one another.

Then Susilaben ignored Ged's mother and addressed Pa. She asked him how he was and she said it quite shyly. Pa said he was well and asked her how she was. She was well, considering. She smoothed the pleats of her sari. She kept looking at the kitchen table, waiting for someone to offer her a seat.

'We were having tea,' Pa said.

Susilaben looked at Pa's face, then she said quickly that her youngest nephew was having his head-shaving ceremony and two of the girl cousins had mumps and couldn't come, and they needed more girls to be goynis.

Pa just stood there.

'When is it?' Mona asked.

'A week today,' Susilaben said, turning to Mona with a grateful look. 'Sunday morning. Please come at eight.'

Mona replied in Gujarati. Auntie, we will have guests in our house on Sunday, she said.

Pa glanced sharply at Mona, then at me. Mona was telling Susilaben that we would have our periods on Sunday so we could not be goynis.

All three of you? Susilaben asked, also in Gujarati.

Mona shrugged to indicate it was out of our hands.

Since she could not stand in our kitchen, with our father watching, and begin an argument with us about our menstrual cycles, Susilaben said simply, in English, 'I see,' and then she turned to Pa. 'It is truly sad about dear Charu.'

She took a step towards Pa and grasped both his hands in hers and did not seem to notice how his face whitened.

'But you know we are at the centre every week. We have been there all this time. We understand how it is, but it's been long enough.'

Pa withdrew his hands.

'It is kind of you to remember the children. You are welcome to come again,' he said.

Mona showed Susilaben out.

We heard Susilaben whisper in the hallway, 'Does Ranjan know?'

She was talking about Ged's mother.

'Know what, Auntie?' Mona said, and Susilaben made a jumbled reply and left.

When Mona returned to the kitchen, Pa and Ged's mother were standing in the doorway looking into the garden with their cigarettes lit. He was explaining to Ged's mother about the community and the community centre.

'It's like any place where people assemble believing they are the same,' he was saying. 'You cannot think your own thoughts.'

Mona stared at Pa's back. Then she went upstairs. She didn't come down again until Ged's mother had gone. We put Ged's mother's lasagne in the freezer and cooked rice. While Pa was writing to Bala after dinner, Mona kept switching channels on the radio in between cleaning and putting things away. She began scrubbing old burned dal from the top of the cooker.

After ten minutes of this, she turned the radio down, and we knew she was going to start on Pa. I went to the bathroom. I sat on the closed lid of the toilet and visualised Durham and Cleveland: the trees and snow outside, and then the infinite line of courts inside. I imagined the girls I would play. I had already imagined their whole lives and how with every year that they had been training, things had been stacking up against me. But it wouldn't matter. Years of skipping and ghosting and running wouldn't matter once we were on the court and they were breaking their rackets against the walls. There was one girl I'd imagined who was thirteen. She lived with her father. Her father had taken her out of school when she was an infant and had been training her ever since. He had her skip with a skipping rope for an hour in the morning and an hour in the evening. While she was playing, her father made signs to her that only she could understand. She would be successful at Durham and Cleveland. She would win every match she played with ease until she got to me. Nobody would think I had a chance. I'd enter the court and Pa would tell me to do my best and he would go and stand next to the girl's father. At first it would all go her way. She'd take nearly every point, but then she'd get ahead of herself. She'd be at five and already seeing nine, and that was when I'd slow things down, hitting drives that clung to the wall. She'd get to the ball, but with each swing, she would fear breaking her racket and this thought would paralyse her. She would look at her father for direction and he would shake his head. She would begin talking herself out of the game, and all I had to do was stay in it.

'We can't always do whatever we like,' Mona was telling Pa when I returned to the kitchen. 'What do you want us to say to Aunt Ranjan when she calls?'

I sat next to Pa. It was embarrassing, because Mona and Pa were completely quiet and they were looking at each other, Pa with his pen in his hand, Mona with her scouring pad. He put the pen down.

'What are we talking about?' he said very gently.

And abruptly, Mona gave it up.

'It doesn't matter,' she said. 'Never mind.'

Pa went back to his letter.

'What about tomorrow, Pa?' Mona asked, after a while.

When there was no reply, she murmured, 'Pa.'

Pa looked up again.

'Did you hear me?' she asked.

Pa thought about it. 'What about tomorrow,' he repeated.

Mona waited.

'The cash and carry,' she said at last. 'We have to go tomorrow.'

'I said we will go,' Pa replied coolly and went back to his writing.

Mona stared at him. Her eyes were bright with tears. 'No you didn't.'

She was half accusing him, half pleading with him. Pa's pen stalled and his face held such a pained, helpless expression that once again Mona's attack floundered. She turned away from him and flicked the switch on the extractor hood. The sound of it drowned out her scrubbing and anything Pa could have said.

While we were still finishing up in the kitchen, Pa signed his letter and folded it into its envelope. Then he went out into the hallway to leave the envelope by the door. We listened to him climbing the stairs. Mona began wiping the sink. Khush haphazardly swept sections of the floor. I said I had left my rucksack in the car.

For the rest of the night, Mona wanted to talk about Pa. She said that he knew we couldn't keep running to the VG store every time we needed something because at some point we weren't going to be able to afford it. She talked about the cash and carry for a while. And then she got onto the subject of Pa's work. Khush said it was always quieter in the summer and Mona said no, it wasn't. She said he was letting his customers down by missing appointments and even though people felt sympathy for his circumstances, they weren't going to forget that their lights were out or their fridges were broken, and no one came. No one was going to forget that when they needed him, Pa was at Western Lane.

On a long cold day at the end of July, Pa and Ged's mother were up on the balcony while Ged and I were resting on the bench below them. We had a small plastic cup of lemonade each, from a flask Ged's mother had given us. We had finished a game and were supposed to sprint outside before I trained with Pa, but it was late and we were hungry and we just sat on the bench. The lemonade was super. Cold, with sharp bubbles that came up into your nose and tingled inside your stomach. Pa and Ged's mother couldn't see us under the balcony. They didn't know we were there.

Pa began talking about his work, and how there seemed to be no end to it. You could tell he was leading up to something and he was doing it slowly because he didn't know what it was yet.

I could have stood up then, made any sort of noise, and Pa would have stopped, but I didn't, and nor did Ged. We drank our lemonade and listened. We were aware of our own breathing and the cold tingling taste of our drinks.

In truth, Pa said very little. He was silent for long stretches. After one of these silences, we heard Pa asking Ged's mother if she didn't feel, sometimes, that there was too much time. He asked her if things terrorised her, like hours, or the expressions on a child's face, or the clattering of lids on pans.

Maybe she moved in some way that told Pa she understood.

He was quiet, and then he said: 'The children. The girls. Sometimes I look at them and I think they will eat me.'

His voice was calm. Sitting below him, I felt that some unpleasant sound would come down on us next, something that had been inside Pa for a long time, but there wasn't anything. I think they will eat me.

We listened to Pa's steps descending the back stairway, followed by Ged's mother's steps, and then they were outside. We could see them through the glass of the double doors, and by the way they stood facing out, we knew they were smoking. Ged turned his head to look at the grip on my racket. I had asked him earlier if he would check it for me because it was already in bad shape. He took it and began taping it. I put my cup of lemonade on the floor next to my feet and got up. I saw Ged glance towards the double doors. I stood on one foot, holding the other foot back to stretch my quad. I thought that in a minute Ged would give me my racket and tell me he had better get back to work, but he stayed where he was.

When Pa and Ged's mother came inside, their faces were bright and they looked relaxed. You couldn't know that only minutes ago Pa had said probably the saddest thing he'd said out loud in his whole life, and we had heard him. Ged's mother was wearing her red raincoat. She held both her gloves in one hand.

'Did you like the lemonade?' she asked me.

'It was really good,' I said. 'Thank you.'

The tip of her nose was bright. She smelled of something sweet. I let my foot down. I was shivering. Ged got up from the bench, and then he gave me my racket and went into the court next to ours.

Pa opened the door to our court and I followed him. We warmed up the ball with easy drives and a few volleys. There was a strange feeling in my body, a precariousness; the precariousness you feel inside a dream where you are guilty of something.

Pa stood for a moment with the ball in his hand.

He said, 'A game.'

Pa and I had not played a game in months. I took my place. Pa served a high drifting lob close to the wall, and then gradually drew me into one long rally in which I was beaten, followed by another. He didn't hit hard, but he held the T and made me move. He gave me no time to think. I wasn't thinking. I don't know what happened. I was moving, stepping into my backhand, turning my shoulder with my racket up, when I heard Pa's voice very close to me, calm and clear, and suddenly the whole court was tilting, the air throbbing, and everything was covered in a mist of red.

I knew where I was and where Pa was in relation to me when I let my racket arm fly. I was far enough from the backhand corner to strike well, and Pa was at a diagonal from me. I can see him even now, on the T, body open, face turned towards me to check my position. But at the time, I wasn't seeing him from that angle. I saw him and myself from above. I had my whole body behind my racket, so that when the ball made contact with his jawbone there was such a resounding crack that you might have imagined for a second that the ball had passed right through him and split against the side wall.

Outside the court I kept saying to Pa that I was sorry, and that it wasn't me, and then I was saying it to Ged's mother. They were sitting on the bench. She was tending to his jaw with ice from behind the bar, wrapped in a thin towel.

She said, 'It's okay, pet,' but her voice was shaking and she didn't look at me. Even she understood enough about the game to recognise that Pa had been standing well out of the way of any stroke I should have played.

Ged got my racket from the service box where I had dropped it. He stood at my side. His face was dark. When he handed me my racket, our fingers didn't touch, but somehow it was the same as when we stepped off the Twister, only this time the thing that moved between us came from him.

I heard Pa tell Ged's mother that he was fine and she said I know. His face was swollen terribly, he could hardly move his mouth, and I thought, How could he be fine. He said we should go home. We got ready to go but I couldn't move from where I was standing.

Ged was still next to me.

He said quietly, 'See you tomorrow.'

'See you,' I said.

Ged's mother looked at me and then Ged. I could see she wanted to go upstairs and she wanted Ged to go with her.

Pa saw it too.

He hadn't spoken to me since I'd hit him, but now he said, his voice gentle and slow and unrecognisable, 'Your backhand's improved.'

He laid his arm over my shoulders and we walked out of the sports centre.

With his words, Pa was telling Ged's mother that what had happened was between me and him, and with the gentleness in his voice he was telling me to calm my mind.

Outside, the sky was mostly dark but there was a low bright whitish band of light at the horizon. I imagined Ged standing out here in a few hours, when the sky would be black everywhere.

Pa's arm was heavy on me. We approached the car and he let his arm fall. He opened the boot of the car so I could put my rucksack inside.

'Do not let your emotions control you when you are on the court,' he said as he closed the boot. The effort to speak made him wince.

It wasn't fully dark when Pa and I reached home, and the bright band of light was still visible. I closed the passenger door and would have got my rucksack, but Pa was standing staring at the house as if I wasn't there, as if, in a minute, he might get back in the car and drive away. I called to him and when he didn't answer me I told him I was going to the shop for milk. I wouldn't be long. He wasn't watching which way I went but I headed in the direction of the VG store anyway, and from there I took the long way around to the hill behind the house. I sat at the foot of the hill. I stayed there until the sky was black and so was the hill behind me and the back of our house and everything existed in one plane, all at once.

See you tomorrow, I whispered.

Six

Pa believed in ghosting, and so did I. When you simulated the movement of the game with your racket, but without the ball, with speed and intent, over and over, it was more than a rehearsal or a drill. Sometimes I thought it was more than the game itself. Pa watched us, and I paid more attention to my footwork then. I played my strokes more fully. I pressed into the follow-through before stepping off. And then Pa told us we must push harder. He told us that when we were ghosting, we must play our strokes with care, but we must also imagine that we were playing a real game with all its urgency. That we were up against Jahangir. That was when the whole thing changed. I began to feel the physical pressure of the movements and could predict where and when the pain in my body would come. Often, it only felt painful and difficult, but other times I had a rhythm, and then something more than a rhythm. My body became weightless. The surfaces and dimensions of the court were clear to me and I knew my place within them while feeling, at the same time, that I was nowhere.

After I hit Pa, Ged's mother stopped Ged training with me.

For a week, I looked for him at Western Lane but he wasn't there. Pa and Ged's mother met and smoked as usual, and as I watched them talking outside, I knew. At first Pa didn't say anything. He fed the ball to me and took me through my drills, and after a few days he said my sisters would have to spend more time training with me before the tournament. Then he told me that Ged's mother didn't like what had happened on the court. We were in the car driving home. I was holding my racket between my knees, and I knew I was going to be sick in the space in front of the passenger seat.

'Isn't he coming back?' I asked. Pa must have heard something in my voice because he stopped the car.

'Open the window,' he said, and I did. Then he said, 'He's coming back, but you won't practise with him.'

'Didn't you tell her?' I cried.

'Tell her what?'

'That it would be okay with Ged. I mean, it would be safe.'

'Would it?' Pa said gently.

The bruising on Pa's face was dark yellow with the breaking down of the blood that had pooled under his skin. I couldn't look at him.

At night, Khush came into my bed and told me to sit up. She started tying and untying my short hair in small tight plaits. It made me sleepy. She told me to go and brush my teeth and when I came back she started on my hair again and I fell asleep when it was half done.

At Western Lane, Pa came into the court more often than before. I felt that he was watching me more closely.

Once, I was hitting volleys when my shoulder twinged. I put my arm down quickly and began to drive.

'You have to warm up properly,' Pa said from the back of the court.

'I did warm up.'

Pa came forward and I could smell the staleness in his breath and was surprised that he could not. Then I wasn't sure if it was his breath or mine.

'What do you want to do?' he said.

'I want to play,' I said, and because he didn't answer and his face looked so tired I said, 'We could ghost.'

Pa climbed the stairs to the balcony. I pushed the ball to the tin with my foot and waited. When Pa did not instruct me, I turned.

'You know what to do,' he said from the balcony.

I let my racket head drop. Pa wanted me to ghost on my own.

I went to the front of the court and took the timer from the pocket of my rucksack. I set it and stood on the T. I kept my eyes on the red line on the front wall. I resisted the impulse to turn again to look at Pa. When you ghost without instruction, it is extremely hard, mentally, to begin, and even harder to continue. Pa knew this. He knew what he was doing.

The timer buzzed. With my racket up, I made the first split step towards the back of the court. I ghosted for thirty seconds to my forehand side, rested ten seconds on the T, increased the pace. I did the same on the backhand before moving to the front of the court, and only then did I have anything like a rhythm.

It was after the fourth or fifth cycle that I fell against the wall. It was after the seventh that I heard Pa telling me to stop. I was feeling light, and everything was beginning to drift. I couldn't hear the timer. Something was happening inside the court. I felt the steady momentum in my body that meant my swing should have made a clean arc, but my racket was moving uneasily in space. The air was warping around it and I kept extending my body.

'Stop it.'

I didn't know how to stop it.

Pa's hand was on my shoulder. He was crouching in front of me, lifting the racket from my closed fist.

'You can stop,' he said.

He placed the racket gently on the floor. He looked so tired.

'I'm tired,' I said. My heart was beating hard.

'I know.'

Pa got up, collected my things from the front of the court. When he was by the door, he hovered there. I picked up my racket. I heard my father breathing, felt the grip of my racket in my hand.

And then a slow beating sound that was not my heart rose up somewhere.

It was a solid sound. Deep, familiar. It seemed to be both inside me and out.

It was Ged.

He was in the next-door court, hitting a ball.

I looked at the wall between our court and Ged's. I looked at Pa. Pa opened his mouth. Before he could say anything, I lowered my racket and went to him. He pulled the door shut behind us, turning the latch. Ged was still playing next door.

'Do you want water?' Pa asked.

'No.'

He lifted my rucksack on his shoulder.

'I'll wait in the car,' he said. He hesitated, and added, 'Don't sit in your damp clothes.'

I stood in the corridor. I listened to Ged and to the usual sounds from the swimming pool. Eventually Ged came out of his court, and we sat on the bench.

'Are you okay?' he asked.

'I miss playing.'

He leaned forward. He tapped down the strings on his racket.

'My mum just needs time,' he said.

'She thinks I'll hit you.'

'I don't know. Maybe it's what she thinks.'

'I won't.'

He put his racket on the bench next to him. 'I know,' he said.

He sounded so sure.

He turned his head to look at me. We heard Maqsud's voice upstairs. I thought about Durham and Cleveland in January. Red berries on trees, frost shimmering on rooftops.

'At school, we're playing a computer game,' I said. 'It's called *The Oregon Trail.* We're pioneers travelling from Missouri to Oregon in wagons and we don't know if we're going to survive. We have to make decisions about food and weapons. We visit forts to trade and we hunt and cross rivers, and the computer tells us how we're doing. Sometimes it snows. You get a tombstone scene if someone dies.'

My hand was in Ged's. I felt the tip of his thumb on my palm.

I was going to tell him more. I was going to tell him that our whole year had to play the computer game but our teacher, Miss Holloway, didn't like it. She thought it didn't teach us enough. She kept stopping us and telling us to switch the computers off so that she could read to us about the lives of Native American Indians. She had a book about Indian chiefs and all the treaties they had made giving up their land. She wanted us to try to understand why they made those treaties. Some of the children turned in their seats to look at me whenever Miss Holloway talked about Indians. I blushed under their stares, which convinced them that whatever they had imagined was true. Miss Holloway's book of chiefs was sadder than the game. Black Elk was the saddest. 'I did not know then how much was ended,' Black Elk said. 'When I look back now from this high hill of my old age . . . I can see . . . the nation's hoop is broken and scattered. There is no centre any longer . . .' It had nothing to do with me and it made me so sad I started crying at my desk and Miss Holloway had to stop reading.

I felt tears coming now. Probably I should have kept talking, because in the quiet I began thinking about the funfair and Mona telling us that Ged and his mother were only in our lives because Ma was dead.

I tried to remember Ma's face. I looked at the blank walls of the court.

I kept my hand in Ged's and my shame was as big as the sky.

Outside, Pa was by the car with Ged's mother. He was pointing something out to her, towards the trees on the other side of the running track, and she was smiling. They put their cigarettes out.

'Hello, pet,' Ged's mother said.

When I didn't answer right away she looked at the gravel at our feet. I saw that she felt bad.

I moved my racket from my right hand to my left and stepped towards her.

'Please, I'd really like to play Ged again,' I said.

Ged's mother raised her eyes to mine.

'No, love,' she said.

'Please.'

Pa lifted my racket from my hand and went to the back of the car to put the racket inside.

'Sweetheart,' Ged's mother said. Her voice was kind and sad. 'Look at your father's face.'

The bruising on Pa's jaw was still dark yellow. Sickly green in some light. Ged's mother spoke really gently, as if she was pleading with me, and I knew she only wanted me to understand, but what she had said seemed cruel to me and maybe she felt it too because then she put out her hand and said, 'I'm sorry, love.'

'I wouldn't hurt Ged,' I said.

'I don't think you would, but I don't know.'

She glanced at Pa and I felt Pa looking at both of us. Ged's mother put her hands inside her coat pockets, getting ready to go inside. She had denied me the only thing I wanted, but standing there in the car park I just kept thinking that she was a nice person.

'You don't have to go,' I said to her.

Tears came into her eyes. She smiled at me. She looked at her watch.

'I'd better.'

She said see you to Pa and then bye to me.

Pa and I got in the car, and from the road I twisted round in my seat to look back at Western Lane. The sports centre stood under the dark grey sky, bathed in yellow light.

That night we could hear the radiators knocking again. It was cold. My sisters went to bed early and I sat with Pa in the living room watching Bala's video. Pa was on the comfortable chair at an angle to the TV, opposite Ma's chair, and I was at the far end of the sofa. He kept glancing at me.

'It is good to have someone with whom you can talk,' he said, eventually.

I kept my eyes on the TV.

'About what?' I said.

I didn't know if he wanted to talk about me and Ged or himself and Ged's mother but I didn't want to talk about either.

Pa turned the TV down.

I felt him waiting for me to look at him, and when I did there must have been something terrible in my expression because some creature, limping and friendly, behind his eyes, seemed to back away.

He looked confused and then he replied.

'It doesn't always matter what you talk about,' he said.

I felt myself agreeing with him inside. Then I thought of the cold tingle of Ged's mother's lemonade in my stomach as Pa stood on the balcony above us telling her about the things that terrorised him.

'But sometimes it does matter?' I said.

I didn't know, then, that it was to the limping creature behind Pa's eyes that I should have been paying attention. Instead, I was thinking of the presence whose hold on Pa was slipping away, and the feeling that if it did, then our living room and our house and Western Lane and everything we knew would go with it.

'Do you remember Ma?' I asked.

We could hear water running and doors opening and closing upstairs as my sisters moved between the bathroom and bedroom. Pa's face became very dark and then pale. He turned the TV up. We watched the game on the screen in silence. My body felt weak, almost wobbly. I suddenly wanted to forget everything and just talk to Pa about the game.

Jahangir Khan was playing Qamar Zaman. Zaman could hit better than anyone.

Before playing Qamar Zaman in the 1975 Open, Geoff Hunt had omitted him from the list of men he considered challengers. After playing him, Geoff Hunt came off the court a beaten man, saying, 'I can't speak.' It had made a headline, which Maqsud had kept in a folder that he showed to me and Ged. On our TV, Jahangir Khan was going to defeat Qamar Zaman in three games.

I turned to Pa, and whatever I was going to say died on my lips. Pa was looking at Ma's chair. He wasn't staring.

His expression was calm. The dark bruise on his jaw was like a hole in the middle of his face.

'Pa,' I said.

He kept looking at Ma's chair.

I had asked him if he remembered Ma and again I tried to remember, but all I could see were insignificant things. The height of her. Her arms on the arms of her chair, bent at the elbows. The dust that blackened the soles of her feet.

'I'm going to go up,' I said.

Pa turned his head, not to me, but to the TV. Sometimes, when Qamar Zaman played, his shots were so perfect and unexpected that they could make you forget whatever you had been thinking.

Upstairs, my sisters and I lay in our beds in the dark, quiet but awake. Pa must have switched the TV off or muted the sound because it was quiet downstairs too, except for his voice. Every now and then we heard it. It came up from the living room directly below us, which meant that he wasn't speaking to a person on the end of the telephone in the hallway but to someone in the room with him.

I lifted my head. I could make out the bundle that was Khush in her bed, her pale face hovering above the covers.

I got up onto one elbow. 'I think he's—'

'Shh.' Mona shifted her body in the bed above me as if she was going to get down.

'What is it?' Khush whispered to me.

'I think . . . I don't know,' I said.

'You do know. What was Pa saying to you?'

Her voice was pushing at me in a way that I didn't like.

'He wasn't saying anything.'

'It must have been something,' Mona said, shifting again. 'We could hear you getting upset.'

'We were just watching the game,' I said.

I put my head back on the pillow. My sisters and I listened to the sounds from downstairs. I closed my eyes. I tried to imagine Ma climbing the stairs. I tried to imagine her milky breath entering the room. Her voice telling us to sleep. But it came to nothing because there, in the dark, plainer than all of this, was the feeling of someone's thumb on my palm.

None of us went down to Pa that night or any of the nights that followed.

We began to recognise Ma's presence in our house, not through any experience of her – there was no sound, or touch, or change in the air – but through the quality of Pa's attention. His eyes were bright. He would look at things, and we'd know that his attention was on her, that he was listening to her. Sometimes, watching TV, he forgot, and we watched for the change that would come over him when he remembered.

We felt him waiting for us to go to bed, and we didn't know if it was because he wanted us to go or because he didn't. We thought that maybe it would be better if we stayed downstairs with him, but when one night we made it clear that this was what we intended, he simply stood up and went to bed, leaving us alone in the living room.

We sat where we were in front of the TV. We tried not to fall asleep. We wanted to go upstairs but we didn't dare to move. Eventually I asked Khush if she could see Ma. Khush shook her head.

'It's not her,' she said.

After school one afternoon, Mona insisted we go with her to the hair salon where she used to work. The manager looked surprised and upset seeing her in her school uniform, and us with her. He kept staring at our grey and yellow ties. Mona said to him she wanted a haircut. We were surprised at this because she hadn't said why she wanted to go in there. We thought maybe she wanted her job back or was owed money. None of us had ever had our hair cut in a salon before. The manager said, I don't know. He spoke in a hushed, anxious voice. Mona said she wanted a haircut, that was all. You could tell the manager felt sorry for us but it was embarrassing for him seeing that Mona, who had been doing all his paperwork, was only a child.

Khush and I sat on a sofa by the window and watched while Mona got her hair washed and then trimmed a little and then blow-dried. The manager did it himself. He was very slow and careful. Mona was looking in the mirror the whole time. She was holding back tears. When it was done, the manager brushed away the hair on her shoulders, briskly but lightly. Then she and the manager went to the counter together. The manager looked embarrassed all over again when she searched in her school bag for the money to pay him. He put the money in the till. Mona waited for him to meet her eyes and then she said thank you, as if he had done something extraordinary, and he nodded. He came to the door with us and stood there as we walked off down the road.

Pa began waking early and leaving the house at eight in the morning and returning home after us, the way he did when he was going to work. Mona found out that he was in fact working, some of the time. We imagined that the rest of the time he was walking around outside. He came home with his hands frozen and frost clinging to the shoulders of his coat. Whatever he was doing, it seemed to be making him sick. His face was different. His hands shook sometimes when he poured boiling water from the kettle. Mona was worried that Pa was going to break down and tell someone about his seeing Ma in our living room. She ran to the telephone whenever it rang so that she could explain to whoever was calling that Pa was unavailable, that he was at work or otherwise occupied.

But I knew Pa wasn't going to tell anyone anything, because he was completely alone.

I started staying up with Pa after my sisters went to bed. He and I sat in the living room with Bala's video playing on the TV.

'Can't you stop, Pa?' I whispered to him.

I didn't think he could hear me.

I suppose I was trying to ask him if he could stop remembering, if he could come back to Western Lane and talk to Ged's mother up on the balcony or wherever he wanted, if everything could be like before.

Eventually one night he fixed his gaze on Ma's chair and said, 'I can't.'

I didn't know if he was trying to answer me or Ma. I thought of the sad horse in the funfair with its itching hoof and the flies buzzing around its head. Pa had to grip the arms of his chair to push himself up to stand and even then you could see it was an effort. He went upstairs, leaving me in the living room by myself.

Ma's chair had one leg that was darker than the others, where Pa had had to fix it. I had forgotten which leg, and the difference was so slight that with only the light from the TV it was difficult to tell. I got up quickly to switch on the main light and then I stepped out of the living room, closing the door behind me to keep the heat in. I stood in the quiet of the hallway and phoned Uncle Pavan.

Seven

Pa told us there are times when a player needs help from outside. He said in part this is because the player can't see all that's happening on the court, and he said Jahangir Khan understood this well. In his 1980 match in Karachi against Qamar Zaman, Jahangir Khan's coach, Rahmat, told him to answer everything Qamar Zaman did with length: shot after shot to the back of the court. Jahangir was only sixteen. He got nervous and allowed Qamar Zaman to take the first game, and when he also took the second, Rahmat told Jahangir not to worry about the result any more, but just to show him what he'd done in their last training session. Qamar Zaman lost the third game and the fourth. In the fifth game, Qamar Zaman was fighting back and the score was 6–6. Rahmat showed the sixteen-year-old Jahangir a clenched fist, telling him to stay steady, and he indicated that the control on Qamar Zaman's forehand was breaking down, and he should play the ball there. Jahangir followed his coach's instructions. In response, Qamar Zaman hit the tin repeatedly and this time he was unable to come back. Jahangir Khan wrote all this down in a book. I imagined him and Rahmat going over and over everything in order to choose what was important to record.

We were in the kitchen when they came. Aunt Ranjan's voice in the hallway announced their arrival like a ship's horn and my sisters glanced at me and one another in surprise. Mona got up to wash her hands. She was drying them on a tea towel when Aunt Ranjan swept in with Pa and Uncle Pavan following behind.

As soon as she stopped in our kitchen, we saw how much it lacked. There was no hot food, no tins or Tupperware on the side, no sign of activity or warmth. It wasn't just that we weren't ready for visitors. It was everything.

Aunt Ranjan let Pa through while she took in the situation.

'You didn't tell them we were coming,' she said.

Pa sat down.

'I'm sorry, Aunt Ranjan,' Mona said. 'It's our fault. We thought you'd be later with all the traffic. Are you hungry?'

Khush and I stood up so that Aunt Ranjan and Uncle Pavan could sit with Pa. Aunt Ranjan threw Mona a sceptical look.

'Tea will do for now,' she said, and sent me to get the stool from our room and the chair from Pa's.

Near the end of our phone call, I had told Uncle Pavan

that Pa was talking to Ma in the living room. I said it was because of me and now Pa was sick from it. Uncle Pavan was quiet. After a minute he moved something, like a water glass, from one spot on the phone table to another, and said, 'You know I have to tell your aunt Ranjan?' I could feel that Uncle Pavan was worried about this. 'It's okay,' I said. 'I know.'

Over tea, and later, while she fried parathas on our stove and served dinner close to midnight, I waited for Aunt Ranjan to tell Pa that I had asked Uncle Pavan to come, but she didn't. She didn't say very much at all. She kept looking at Pa's face, and whenever she went into the living room she made Uncle Pavan go in with her. We too watched Pa. We saw that he was comforted when Uncle Pavan was near.

I went to the bathroom to wash my hands after dinner and on my way back I met Uncle Pavan standing in the doorway into the living room with such a downcast, disappointed look on his face that I wanted to go to him and tell him not to worry, that Ma would be back, it was just that there were so many people. But inside me I heard Khush's voice saying it wasn't going to be Ma, and I went into the kitchen.

Pa and Uncle Pavan were to sleep in Pa's room, and Aunt Ranjan would be in our room with us. My sisters and I made excuses to stay up. We asked Aunt Ranjan if she would make us warm milk with saffron and sugar. Mona found the saffron behind the tea bags. Khush got out the playing cards and we played a few hands until Aunt Ranjan said she was too tired and went to bed, telling us to wash our cups and not just leave them in the sink. While my sisters and I were in the kitchen, we heard Uncle Pavan and Pa talking and then Uncle Pavan came in with his boots and coat on and told us that he and Pa were going outside for a walk. We waited for him to tell us we should go to bed, but he just stood for a minute and then turned around and went to the hallway to get Pa's coat.

We poured ourselves glasses of water and hung around downstairs, but we must have drifted upstairs at some point and climbed into our beds and fallen asleep. When we woke it was light and we could hear Aunt Ranjan and Pa talking in the kitchen.

We brushed our teeth, washed, and went down.

There was a strong smell of incense from the living room. Mona made a face as we passed the door, and when we looked in we saw the windows were open and there was a new tulsi plant on the wall unit.

Pa and Aunt Ranjan were at the kitchen table. Pa was dressed in his suit with a cup of coffee in his hands. Breakfast was laid out and it was warm because all the radiators were on. Aunt Ranjan wished us good morning and got to her feet, saying they had already eaten and that Pa and Uncle Pavan had fixed the heating. She went into the garden to join Uncle Pavan. The three of us moved as one to stand in front of the radiator. Our bodies pressed against it and we felt bereft and didn't care that our legs burned. We didn't think Pa could have gone to bed, but he had showered and shaved his face. He watched us. We sat down to eat what Aunt Ranjan had made. When we were finished, Pa told me to get my things. We were going to Western Lane.

It was just me and him. He stood outside the court with his coat on and instructed me. He had me sprint for a few minutes until I was warm. Then he told me to set my own drill. I kept it simple and slow. Drives, followed by drops.

'Good,' he said. His voice was thick. He sounded almost surprised. I thought that what had surprised him was the drills I had chosen. There was nothing much to them, but I was capable of doing them well.

I kept going, keeping everything steady.

After several drills, Pa said, 'Come out.'

It was the same thick voice. It seemed to cover me. We sat on the bench and I tried to quieten my breathing.

Pa said, 'You like your uncle.'

I didn't know if it was a question. I replied, 'I like him a lot,' and I knew I had done the right thing when Pa's voice thickened again.

'It has been hard for you, since Ma . . .'

I sat very close to him and we listened to doors opening and closing upstairs.

He tried again. 'It has been hard . . . It is hard . . .'

'Pa?'

He let me rest my cheek against his arm, even moved closer so that it would be comfortable. The cloth of his ulster coat was rough but warm. When he breathed, my body rose and fell with his.

'Your uncle and aunt,' he said.

Our bodies rose with his breath. 'Your aunt and uncle would like you to go with them, to live with them in Edinburgh.'

I didn't move. Because if I moved, then something covering us would begin to slide off.

'. . . in Edinburgh . . . if you . . .'

Pa's shoulder fell back as he began to turn towards me, and I had to lift my head.

I knew he was going to tell me it was up to me, and I knew that if I said yes, then we would be close again. But I was already answering him.

'You said it was good to have someone to talk to,' I was saying. 'You were supposed to talk to Uncle Pavan. There was nothing about Edinburgh. You—'

I put my hand over my mouth. Pa cleared his throat.

'Your aunt and uncle wanted to have children. They wanted it very much. But you see they couldn't . . . My brother, your uncle . . . It will be better for you. You will still be my child. You know that.'

And, impossibly, his voice was covering me once more. I heard Ged's mother humming through the open door of the bar upstairs, but Pa didn't, because he was looking at me. He was saying, 'You will be their child as well as mine,' and, 'It's up to you.'

I rested my head on his arm again. I heard the scraping of chair legs upstairs and then I heard Ged's voice and the whirring drone of his mother's vacuum going back and forth on the floor of the balcony. I felt drowsy.

'What about Durham and Cleveland?' I asked. Though my voice was taken by the whirring noises above us, Pa heard. I don't know if he was quiet or if he told me I would have to talk to Uncle Pavan about it. I remember both.

Aunt Ranjan was making pani puris. She had sent Uncle Pavan to the cash and carry and he had returned with a car boot full of food. A sack of flour, a tin of oil, rice, lentils and enough fresh food for a week. Khush was in front of the stove next to Aunt Ranjan, who was teaching her how to get the puris the right colour in the frying pan. The windows were steamed up because Aunt Ranjan had three big pans on the go, boiling water. She had Mona rolling the dough for the puris and cutting it into rounds with the rim of a metal bowl.

Aunt Ranjan glanced at me and Pa when we came in.

'You're back,' she said to us, and to Khush she said, 'I'll teach your sister now. You chop the mint over there for the pani.'

Khush put the frying spoon on a saucer. The way she and Mona looked at me, I knew they knew why Pa had taken me out. I thought Aunt Ranjan would want to go and talk to Pa to see how it had gone, but she just stayed where she was and showed me what to do.

The tiny puris puffed up into balls as soon as you slid them into the oil and if one didn't puff up you only had to nudge it with the frying spoon on one side and then the other. You had to keep flipping the puris over until they were golden brown and then wait a bit before taking them out. You had to concentrate if you wanted them all to come out the same colour. While I stood frying the puris, I felt Pa watching me. He was standing with his shoulder against the frame of the door, talking to Uncle Pavan, who was drinking tea at the table. It was the same closeness I had felt between us on the bench at Western Lane. In the kitchen, he and I were separate from my sisters and Aunt Ranjan and Uncle Pavan, and it was because I was leaving him.

We took five puris at a time onto our plates. We had to fill each one ourselves, gently tapping a hole into the top with the end of a spoon. When the hole was the right size, we slid in cubes of potato, a few chickpeas, some mung beans, chopped onions and coriander. Then we added chutney and poured in as much pani as the puri would hold before putting the whole thing in our mouths. Uncle Pavan praised us because the puris were crispy inside and out and made a good cracking sound when we tapped them with our spoons. Pa put more puris on my plate and filled my glass with Coke, and everything he gave me, I finished.

'What did you do to Pa?' Mona whispered when we were in our beds and Aunt Ranjan and Uncle Pavan were downstairs with Pa. She was on her stomach, with her head hanging over the side of her bunk to address me. 'We heard them talking.'

Khush climbed out of her bed and into mine. She pushed Mona's face away. I listened to Khush breathing softly.

'It doesn't matter what you did. It's not your fault. You don't have to go with them,' she said.

'I didn't do anything,' I said.

Khush brought her hand out from under the covers and touched my hair. She smelled of mint and lemons. I began to cry.

'I already told Pa I would go,' I said.

'You changed your mind. Tell her, Mona.'

Mona slid down from her bed. She put on the main light and knelt next to us.

'She's right. It's not your fault. You don't have to go.'

I looked at both of my sisters. I wanted to tell them again that I hadn't done anything. I wanted to ask them what I had done. I thought of Pa in his coat and his thick voice covering me.

'I already told Pa,' I said.

In the morning, Uncle Pavan asked me if he and I could go for a walk. He said I would have to lead the way. We went up to the high school, where there was a bit of green.

'What do you think?' he said. 'About coming with us? We want you to come very much. We think you'll like it in Edinburgh, but we know it isn't the same.'

'I told Pa I will come,' I said. 'Didn't he tell you?'

'Yes. But I . . . we . . . wanted to know what you thought about it.'

'I don't know.'

'Shall we sit down?'

There was a bench in the middle of a roundabout. Around it the grass was long and wet but the seat was dry.

'That's better,' Uncle Pavan said, and then, 'You know you are very dear to us.'

We watched the traffic. Uncle Pavan put his hands on his knees.

'Your aunt and I are going to go home to get things ready for you. If you want to come then, your pa will bring you.'

I could see he was finding this conversation difficult, and I was about to tell him I did want to come, when he said suddenly, 'Did you know that your ma and pa lived with us, in Edinburgh?'

I stared at him.

'It was before Mona was born. Your ma liked Edinburgh. She liked the mountains.' He laughed. 'The hills above the town. She called them mountains. She liked to walk where she could see them.'

I remembered walking in Edinburgh when we visited

Aunt Ranjan and Uncle Pavan. Ma would be in her sari and her oversized Scholl's, always a few steps behind Pa, her eyes always drifting between the roads and the pavements and the doorways of shops, always looking for us, gathering us in. I tried to imagine her walking without us.

'Oh now,' Uncle Pavan said. He looked for a handkerchief.

'I'm sorry,' I said, blowing my nose. 'I'm not upset. It's just sometimes . . .'

'I know,' Uncle Pavan said.

'You know?'

'Yes. Why not?'

Why not, I repeated to myself. I stuffed Uncle Pavan's handkerchief into my sleeve.

I said I didn't know Ma liked mountains, and Uncle Pavan talked about the mountains for a minute and then I said, 'Maybe we should go back now.'

Uncle Pavan walked fast, staring at the ground in front of him because there was much more he had wanted to say. 'Look, Uncle,' I said, pointing out some wild winter flowers that had come up early. He looked but he didn't really see them and I wished that I hadn't stopped him saying what he wanted to.

I asked Pa to tell Ged's mother I was going away. I asked him to see if she would let me play Ged before I went. He talked to her and he seemed brighter when he came back, but he said Ged's mother didn't want me to play Ged. I told him it was okay. I would go and say goodbye to both of them. Pa stood in the doorway and watched me put my rucksack and racket on my bike.

Ged was sitting on a bench. He had on a dark T-shirt that I didn't remember him wearing before.

The sun was very low outside. I remember that inside, the corridor glowed orange from the light through the glass in the doors. I remember Ged standing up, and the emptying, bruising pain in my chest at the sight of him.

He picked up his racket from the bench. He looked at me. Then he turned and went into the court, and I took a deep, slow breath.

I got my racket.

We were both tired and awkward. We hit deliberately slow balls, trying to be accurate. We wanted to slow everything down. We stumbled and mis-hit, but it didn't matter because we were playing. I kept thinking Ged's mother was going to come out onto the balcony to stop us.

Afterwards my heart did not stop pounding. We stood breathing raggedly, looking at the side wall.

'Will you come to see me in Edinburgh?' I said.

'Yeah.'

'I'll meet you off the train. We'll go to Edinburgh Castle. And the mountains. And there's Durham and Cleveland. Uncle Pavan will bring me, I just have to ask him.'

'Do you want to go to Edinburgh, then?'

'No.'

We looked at the smudges on the wall. The late afternoon light had turned them pale orange and pink.

'It's like one of those caves,' Ged said, and I thought, If we could only stay like this.

The orange and pink colour faded and became grey.

Ged went out into the corridor. After a few seconds I heard the echoing sound of the ball from the other court. I went upstairs to say goodbye to Ged's mother. She hugged me and said she would always be glad to see me.

I saw Maqsud, drinking at one of the tables. I went to him. I told him I was going.

'I know,' he said.

I felt guilty because I hadn't made a special trip to see him.

He put a hand in his coat pocket and brought out a blue marble made of glass.

'This is for you,' he said.

The marble was beautiful. It looked like a ball of blue ice. Inside there were two frozen swirls of white.

'Thank you, Uncle,' I cried, holding the marble on my palm.

'Never mind about thank you,' Maqsud said gruffly. 'Some people who should know better were playing terribly slow balls out there.'

'You were watching?' I whispered.

Maqsud's face was all red. He looked angry, but he wasn't.

'I have ears!' he exclaimed, and told me to be off.

When I went downstairs, Ged was still hitting, and I heard him all the way home.

I didn't go into the house right away. I dropped my bike at the bottom of the hill behind the house and got my jacket from my rucksack. It was almost completely dark and the hill was dark blue. I climbed up and sat on the damp blue grass at the top with my arms around my knees. Our house was all lit up and from my spot on the hill, I could see the half-silhouetted figures of Pa and Mona moving about the kitchen, and Khush up in the bathroom. Khush turned out the bathroom light and a minute later she was downstairs in the kitchen with the others. Pa opened the door into the garden so that a yellow band of light fell on the path, and for a long time he stood looking out. I imagined that if he glanced up, he would see me, a blue smudge on the hill behind his house.

Eight

In the court, your mind is not only on the shot you're about to play and the shot with which your opponent might reply, but on the shots that will follow two, three, four moves ahead. You're watching your opponent's position and the game he or she is playing, making calculations. This is how you choose which way to go. Though your mind is following several paths at once, it's not a splitting but an expansion forwards and backwards in time, and it happens so quickly that it feels like instinct. Sometimes, you don't even know you are thinking.

The Edinburgh house was so quiet that sometimes all I could do inside the silence was think, but all my thoughts were big and far apart. It was like wandering around some vast lonely place with no fence posts or markers. My aunt spent her time in the kitchen, and Uncle Pavan was often in his garden. I had thought Aunt Ranjan would have me help her cook and mend and clean from the beginning, but she and Uncle Pavan must have discussed it and come to an agreement. Left alone, I usually sat at the big table in the living room. It was warmest there. During the day, the sun shone in through the big windows. In the evenings, Uncle Pavan lit a fire in the open hearth.

Sitting close to the fire, I would try over and over again to imagine myself into Pa's and my sisters' lives back home, but my mind would not let me. When I slipped under the covers of my old bed I found that Khush was using it, and I was cramped; when I fought my sisters over the last drop of lemonade, no one fought back or even noticed; when I addressed Pa, he finished his coffee, picked up his radio, and went upstairs, and the notes I hung on the washing line blew away unattended to. But when I imagined Durham and Cleveland it was different. Maqsud had told us that there, in the middle of the badminton hall, was a court with four glass walls, a temporary structure that would be present for a short time and would then be gone. In my imagination I could stand with Pa for hours in front of that glass court. Pa and I gestured with our hands as we talked and bright shadows from Uncle Pavan's fire flickered on the walls around us. In Durham and Cleveland everything was possible because I was supposed to be there.

One evening in those early days, when it had turned especially cold and the embers in the fire were glowing, Uncle Pavan came and stood next to my chair in the living room. I closed the book I was reading because I thought that maybe he wanted to start a conversation, but after standing for a minute he went to talk to Aunt Ranjan. He was gone for an hour and he returned with a portable radio that he said was for me. I could listen to it whenever I wished. I thanked him. I said I didn't have my own radio at home.

He said, 'Come.' He wanted to show me the house.

'I know the house,' I said.

'It's different now,' he said. 'It's your home.'

As he took me around, he said he should have done this sooner. He opened the cabinets containing Aunt Ranjan's china and ornaments, the same cabinets Aunt Ranjan had forbidden my sisters and me from going near whenever we visited, and he gave me things to hold, like Aunt Ranjan's porcelain teacups and a glass paperweight that you could turn upside down to see snow inside.

'Will Aunt Ranjan mind?' I asked.

Uncle Pavan started putting things away. He said, 'She knows, but we don't have to make too much of it in front of her.'

I returned the paperweight to its place and switched on my radio.

Pa and my sisters phoned often. If I was on with them for more than a few minutes, Uncle Pavan would bring me a glass of water, which I would put on the phone table. Khush told me Maqsud and Ged's mother had come to the house and Pa had returned to Western Lane. He was going two or three times a week. I wanted to ask her about Ma. I said, 'What about the living room?' After a silence, she said it was okay, Pa was getting better. Sometimes Pa and I spoke for a long time. He asked me what I thought about this or that. Sometimes on the phone I felt the closeness between us that I had felt before I left. I asked Pa to talk to Aunt Ranjan about Durham and Cleveland, to tell her he wanted me to compete in the tournament. Pa replied that he and my sisters would come at Christmas and he would talk to her then, but a few days before Christmas he got a chest infection and phoned to say it would be better if they didn't come.

Uncle Pavan watched me put the phone down. I knew he wanted me to say something but I couldn't speak, and he must have felt bad for me because that same afternoon, when we had finished setting the Christmas tree on its base and were standing back to see how it looked, he said it was a shame about Christmas, and then he said he would speak to my aunt about the tournament. Later, he came to sit next to me at the table in the living room where I was reading and said maybe it would be better if I spoke to her.

I asked him, 'When?' and he said, 'Why not now?'

Aunt Ranjan was sitting on the kitchen floor with a sort of fine dust in the air around her. She was sifting lentils. There was a metal bowl at her side for the tiny stones she found, and five shallow trays surrounded her. Her shoulders moved back and forth as she worked.

'Aunt Ranjan.'

My aunt paused with her palm on the edge of the bowl and looked at me through the dust.

'Can't I help?' I said.

Aunt Ranjan moved a little to one side. She pulled her sari under her to make a space for me. I stepped between the trays and sat beside her on the floor, and she showed me what to do. Soon I was mirroring her movements and I sensed she was no longer feeling put out by the interruption, maybe she was even pleased. I started telling her about squash. I said it was something Pa had taught us. It was something you had to commit to. It involved discipline and practice and I had my own racket already and there was a court not very far away and it didn't cost too much. Then I told her about Durham and Cleveland. I said that Pa would be there and that it was only two days. Aunt Ranjan kept sifting. I thought she was going to pretend I hadn't spoken. But when she stopped to transfer the sorted lentils to another tray, she looked at me. She put down her tray. She said, 'No.'

I met her gaze. 'Pa let me—'

'I know your father did, but that does not mean it is right.' Aunt Ranjan reached over to empty her metal bowl in the bin, then sat still in the dust. 'It is not right for a girl, for my daughter. I told your uncle. But you already know that. You have come to me because it is important to you, and I am saying no because I made a promise to myself to raise you properly, for your mother's sake, and this promise is important to me. When you are older, maybe you will understand.'

Her face was white. She was upset and she wasn't going to be moved, and I couldn't say anything more about it because now Ma was involved. I brushed dust from my knees and started sifting again.

Over Christmas, I felt Uncle Pavan watching me. He became quiet and withdrawn. He put on his boots and coat and went for long walks outside. And then for a few days, instead of going into his garden when he was home, he sat in the kitchen with Aunt Ranjan. Sometimes they talked, long conversations with big gaps inside them. It was after one of these talks that Uncle Pavan took me out into the garden and we stood under the balcony of what was now my bedroom and looked at his trees. He told me that Aunt Ranjan had agreed I could go to Durham and Cleveland.

'Are you sure?' I asked, and Uncle Pavan said that he was sure. I could compete in the tournament, but there would be no more squash after that. The weeks leading up to the tournament would coincide with my starting school in Edinburgh, and Uncle Pavan told me Aunt Ranjan had agreed I could train during those weeks on the condition that I went before school and with him. I hugged him, and he looked pleased and embarrassed and said he had better go and find his racket.

In the kitchen, Aunt Ranjan had turned the taps all the way to fill the sink. I had it in my head that I would thank her and tell her I wouldn't ask her or my uncle for anything again, but the running water was loud and Aunt Ranjan stood in front of the sink and avoided looking at me, and I understood that her shame at bargaining with Uncle Pavan over what I wanted to do would sit under everything that happened between us from then on.

The courts Uncle Pavan booked were in the basement of the office next to the building where he worked. I told him he didn't have to come into the court with me, I could just practise drills by myself. I was afraid that even hitting a few strokes would kill him, but once I saw Uncle Pavan move I thought: Gogi Alauddin. Gogi was small and Uncle Pavan was big and they weren't much alike, but there was something. In our conferences at Western Lane, Pa, Maqsud, Ged and I had discussed Gogi Alauddin. His weakness was that he was not a powerful hitter. His strengths were his quick thinking, his agility and his touch. He read where the ball was going, and because he placed the ball so well, it didn't matter that he wasn't powerful. He drew his opponents into corners with slow drops and lobs, and the whole court was his.

It seemed to me that despite Uncle Pavan's having put his racket down when he was a boy, he had remembered everything. His body had remembered. From the very first strokes, his movement was deliberate and lovely. We had stepped onto the court without conferring as to what we'd do. To begin with, we just hit. We played loose shots away from the walls, expecting nothing back. Then, seeing what came back, we began to pay attention. We circled each other, figuring each other out, increasing the pressure little by little until we were both stretching for the ball. After some minutes, Uncle Pavan stopped. He was breathing hard. He lowered his racket and looked at me.

'I didn't know,' he said.

I kept thinking about Uncle Pavan in class when I was supposed to be writing an introduction about myself. If I wanted to beat him, I would have to hit with enough pace to make it difficult for him to hit the way he liked to, but I didn't want to beat him. I wanted Uncle Pavan to keep playing his soft, accurate game.

When I returned home from school, I dropped my bag in the hallway and went directly to the kitchen to help Aunt Ranjan. She gave me a plate of oat biscuits. After I had eaten them and washed the plate, she showed me how to strain curd so that the shrikhand she was making would turn out creamy and thick. Maybe she was just the same as usual but I felt there was something new in the way she instructed me. I wondered what Uncle Pavan had said to her.

We ate dinner and cleared up, and then Aunt Ranjan lifted her sewing machine onto the kitchen table and I sat opposite her with my homework. When the telephone rang, Uncle Pavan stepped out of the living room into the hallway and Aunt Ranjan and I listened until it was clear he was talking to Pa. Aunt Ranjan indicated that I could go. I poured a glass of water and took it to Uncle Pavan. I put it on the phone table. Then I went upstairs to Uncle Pavan's and Aunt Ranjan's bedroom, switched on the light and picked up the phone on the nightstand beside their bed.

The three of us talked, Pa standing in the hallway at home, Uncle Pavan downstairs, and I in the bedroom. Uncle Pavan told Pa about the drills we had completed in the morning and we discussed what I needed to work on and how we should pace things and what we should do the next day. Pa asked me if there was anything else I was thinking about. He meant in connection with the tournament. I looked at Aunt Ranjan's white bedspread, tucked in and pulled so tight it was completely smooth, and the slip of embroidered cloth under the phone, white and round, and I began to describe Uncle Pavan's game. Pa must have known all about it, having played with Uncle Pavan when they were boys, but he was quiet and let me tell him.

Aunt Ranjan kept asking me about the sleeping arrangements for the night we would be away. I told her Pa's friend's cousin had space for us. I would sleep with Khush and Mona in the flat with the cousin's wife, and the men would sleep in the restaurant downstairs. Then she began to worry about Uncle Pavan. How would my uncle sleep in a restaurant? The evening before the tournament, Aunt Ranjan heaped pillows and extra blankets in the hallway, and in the morning she got up with us in the dark, cooked porridge and helped us load the car.

The squash club was not in Durham, but in a village in the countryside. When we arrived, there was a low mist above the ground and the sun was very pale, giving the scene an eerie, milky glow. The building was set back from the road with a gravel car park in front. Beyond it was an industrial estate; opposite, a row of terraced houses. Everything was dim and strangely lit.

I looked for Maqsud's dusty Peugeot in the car park. I started describing the car to Uncle Pavan and he listened and then he stopped me. He handed me my rucksack and said gently that the others weren't here yet and we should go inside.

There was a wait to register. We queued along a wall with windows overlooking the car park, and even as we waited the mist thickened so that we could hardly see anything outside, while inside two girls stood in front of us, blocking our view of whatever was ahead. The girls were sisters. They had the same big shoulders and pink blotches on their arms and they both carried Prince bags and two rackets each. The rackets belonging to the younger Prince sister were wooden, the same as Jahangir Khan's. It seemed strange to me how definite some things looked, like those rackets sticking out of the bags, when outside everything looked so mysterious.

After that first day when my sisters and I had come home from London with my teardrop racket, Pa hadn't said anything more about it, and at some point my wooden racket had disappeared. I didn't know if Pa had sold it or given it away or put it somewhere safe so he would always be able to find it if we needed it. I didn't want to look at the Prince sisters' rackets, and I didn't want to look outside because each time the mist lifted and I saw a car drive into the car park, it turned out not to be Maqsud's. Twice, Uncle Pavan said, 'They're coming,' but he couldn't know, any more than I could.

The woman behind the registration desk asked for my name. She ruled a line through it on her list and began to tell me about the tournament, but it had become busy and she had to raise her voice above the voices of people coming and going around us. She said there would be eight girls which was not enough to split into groups, so there would be some older girls, and she wanted to know if that was okay and I said it was and she put a tick against the line she had ruled.

Ged's name was below mine. It was his whole name, which made it seem both more like him and less. I stared at it, and the woman kept talking, and the palm of my hand became warm and began to tremble, and by the time we were supposed to step away from the desk, my palm was sweating and I couldn't move. Uncle Pavan coughed. The woman smiled politely. She clicked her pen. She kept looking at me and then she put down the pen and said to Uncle Pavan, 'It's okay,' and slowly, she repeated the tournament rules.

I don't know how long I stood in the dark in front of the glass court. It had taken me some time to find it because from the changing room there had been no signs for the badminton hall and away from the main corridor there had been no one to ask. By the way the soles of my trainers had slid across it, I had guessed that the floor of the hall was dusty. Now there was a dusty smell.

The court in the middle of the hall looked bigger than an ordinary court. It emitted a pale blue glow and it was hovering an inch above the floor. It looked alien and beautiful and it seemed to me that it had existed forever. I thought that was how I would describe it to Pa but then I thought he must already know how it was and there would be nothing to say.

There was no sound in the badminton hall and the longer I stood, the deeper the silence became. It was unlike the silence I'd grown used to in Edinburgh. This silence seemed alive. I had the feeling that the glass court was here for me, and that it wanted me inside it. It glowed. It made a low electronic sound like a hum. It drew closer to me, and faintly at first and then more clearly I saw every move my body would make inside its walls: I saw the tracks along which I was meant to travel, as if they had been laid down long ago, shimmering and pale. I thought of the boy Jahangir Khan running in the snow in the mountains, and of whoever was watching him.

A boy of about Ged's age entered the hall. He switched on the lights. The court fell back and the tracks that were meant for me disappeared. The boy came and stood next to me. He said the court was actually Perspex and the club was only borrowing it. It had been shipped from the Netherlands in a box. He wasn't really interested in the court. He wanted to check my name against his list. He told me I wasn't supposed to be in the hall. I was supposed to be on Court 2.

I faced the boy. I felt glass inside me, cool walls pressing into my chest and back.

The boy looked at me strangely.

'You know that only the final will be played here?' he said.

I didn't know.

I think there's a glass court inside me, I said. But I wasn't speaking to the boy and he didn't hear me. He was saying something about the final. He wanted to know if I was listening. The air smelled sweet and stale and cold. Barely breathing, I said yes, I was listening. I listened to the boy and as my lungs filled with dust, I saw my father growing old outside the Perspex court, waiting to see if I could play.

*

The main corridor was busy with players, but Court 2 was empty. I put my water bottle in front of the tin. A buzzer buzzed somewhere and low-pitched voices echoed in the corridor. Touching the tips of my fingers to the wall for balance, I stretched my left quad slowly, and then my right, casually searching the viewing gallery above the court. Uncle Pavan had found his way there.

And so had Pa.

It was a shock seeing my father. He looked thin and grey next to Uncle Pavan. His suit hung oddly on his shoulders. But his eyes were sharp and he didn't look weak. He looked physically strong. I removed my hand from the wall and stood upright.

My opponent on Court 2 was the older Prince sister. When she came in, she slammed the door shut, stuck out her hand for me to shake and said loudly, 'Sorry! Good luck,' and I said good luck back, and then she said, 'I'm Maria. My sister's Alexandra,' and the whole time I kept thinking about how Pa had looked strong and whether you could know how someone was from looking at them.

We warmed up and began to play. I began to wonder if there was something wrong with the foundations of the squash club because everything shuddered when Maria moved. Her tread was heavy and loud. She let out an explosive noise whenever she hit. I felt that I was in the middle of a stampede. Maria was everywhere, and I was immobilised. She took the lead from the beginning, but anyone could see how badly we were both playing. Though her strokes were good, she was moving too fast and too directly to the T. She was more or less charging at it. I was afraid of her. I was afraid of her barrelling into me, of being injured and taken off the court with my father watching. I lost the first game, and when we switched sides I looked up at the gallery. Pa's gaze met mine.

He knew I was afraid.

I kept looking at him because he was supposed to signal what I should do, but he looked back at me as if he was the one waiting, and the referee called time.

When it came, Maria's serve was fast and low, and the floor shook as she thundered out of her box. I hit a straight drive to the back of the court, and anticipating a drive in return I moved early and got into place ahead of the bounce. I sat low with my racket arm ready to jerk back, and I waited. Coming in too fast behind me, Maria would have to stop dead once she realised I hadn't hit the ball, and since she would have lost all momentum and would have no line of sight to the ball, I could place it anywhere. Everything slowed. I watched the ball bounce slowly and come up slowly and then it was dropping. I could hear Maria at my back, thundering, thundering, until, instead of stopping dead, she was crashing into me. I stumbled forward, banging onto my knees. My racket clattered across the court. I was stunned and slightly winded and my knees hurt when I took the pressure off them, but I made myself stand up quickly because I was aware that upstairs my father and uncle were on their feet. I collected my racket. Maria kept saying sorry and that she had tried to stop.

Pa and Uncle Pavan remained on their feet for the rest of the match and Maria lost her nerve. She had become afraid of hurting me. We played it out, but we both knew I had beaten her the moment she knocked me down. When we shook hands I told Maria it was my fault and I was sorry. She was surprised. Then something in her relaxed and she nodded.

Upstairs, before Pa could ask me what I thought about what had happened, I said, 'I waited too long.'

He looked at me and I felt so sad and so warm. He said, 'It doesn't matter. She should have stopped.'

My sisters hugged me and inspected my knees to see if they were bruised from my fall. They fussed over everything and chattered about the game I had just played but said nothing about the months we had been apart. Khush's hair stuck to her forehead and cheeks. I remembered all the things that I had saved up to tell her and Mona, and that no longer seemed interesting or even worth mentioning, but it didn't matter because my sisters didn't expect anything from me. They just kept chattering and fussing, until suddenly the atmosphere in the viewing gallery changed. It wasn't much; a subtle falling back of things that had been crowding in.

I knew before I turned that it was Ged.

My sisters made space for him. He had to bend down to hug me and he did it quickly and stepped aside, but afterwards I could still feel it. I could feel it when my sisters fussed over me again and I could feel it when I was watching Ged from the gallery. He was breathing hard, hitting lengths, covering the T. There didn't seem to be anything spectacular in what he was doing, but there was. His opponent didn't know until it was too late how powerfully he was being attacked.

Ged and Shaan won their first and second matches, which meant all three of us would play in the semifinals the following day. Maqsud said it was a shame there were so few girls, but that it would get interesting tomorrow. We ate lunch in the car park. We didn't mind that it was cold and the air was still damp and hazy with mist. Maqsud and Uncle Pavan opened the boots of their cars, and Mona got everyone organised with the food she and Aunt Ranjan had packed. We all ate and everyone talked, except Ged. Mona and Khush tried to include him, but he stood slightly apart from the group as if this wasn't what he had come for.

It was late in the afternoon when Ged and I returned to the car park. Neither of us suggested it. We just glanced at each other and went outside. By then it was turning dark. Because of the mist, the windows of the houses opposite glowed faintly orange but we couldn't see in. I thought of the Perspex court, glowing blue with the dust all around it.

'Did you look in the badminton hall?' Ged asked.

It was like something banging down around us, his mentioning it right then when I was already thinking of it. For a few moments, we were back inside the corridor at Western Lane. I smelled chlorine. Blood pounded in my ears. I didn't hear what Ged said next, and maybe he didn't speak, but slowly Western Lane disappeared and the Perspex court rose up behind us, huge and so luminous that I almost turned my head to look.

Across the road, someone opened the door of one of the houses and a triangle of light fell on the gravel in front of it. Ged shifted a little. Seconds passed. At last, he spoke. 'Have you thought about what happens after this?' he asked quietly.

The night we spent at Maqsud's cousin's place, we held a conference but it was unlike any conference we had held before. The cousin brought plates and plates of food upstairs from the restaurant and after we ate, Pa, Maqsud, Uncle Pavan, Ged and I went outside and walked. It was freezing cold. The sky was purple. Near the horizon was a wide, slanting band of a paler shade, and higher up a darker band, slanting the opposite way, deep indigo. It was beautiful. Lights flickered everywhere, even on the bridges spanning the river. In our conference, we didn't talk about the following day's games. We just walked. We crossed the river over one bridge and crossed back over the next, the soles of our boots echoing on the metal and our frozen breath all around us. There was a moment – we were crossing a suspension bridge – when the bridge was swinging under us, falling, then rising again. There were sudden inches of air under our feet and we had to adjust our strides whenever we took a step. Nobody said anything about it. Ged was next to me, and we both looked ahead of us and kept walking. The lights blinked. Pa lit a cigarette and said something about Jahangir Khan. Then Maqsud, behind us, said a few words about Qamar Zaman. I mentioned Gogi Alauddin and someone, Maqsud or Uncle Pavan, brought out a flask, and we stopped, and everyone drank a little. They let me have some to warm up. It made my throat hot. I thought this was how a wake must feel, both sad and happy, and everyone's throats hot, and all their thoughts touching. I passed the flask to Ged. When the men walked on, we lagged behind a little. We heard the snap of a lighter up ahead and caught a flicker of flame. The bridge dipped. We didn't know if we were moving or still.

After the conference on the bridge I didn't think about the Perspex court until we were driving into the car park in front of the squash club the following morning. There was the mist again and the milky glow of the sun on everything. Uncle Pavan parked the car and sat for a minute and I thought he was thinking about it too, but then he said, 'We'll talk to Aunt Ranjan about your friend.' He meant that he would find a way to let my aunt know that there was no harm in my friendship with Ged and I should be allowed to continue it. I tried to imagine Aunt Ranjan saying, Yes that sounds fine, or letting me meet Ged off the train or even talk to him on the phone. I looked at my uncle. He avoided my look and tugged at his seatbelt. 'Well, we don't know,' he said.

In the squash club, the mood was friendly and excited. People greeted one another and stood talking and drinking coffee in the corridors until it was time for the matches to begin. Maqsud said it was always like this on the second day of a tournament.

But on Court 6, the girl opposite me wasn't interested in being friendly. When I put out my hand, she pretended she hadn't seen it. She rushed the warm-up and the racket spin. We began the match and the first thing she did was deliver a fast, aggressive serve intended to come off the wall right at my body. There was a commotion in the viewing gallery until I side-stepped and volleyed. Then she played low, hard lengths. She wanted a fast game, to be done with me so she could get on with the final. I sensed her dismissal of me and was beginning to feel oppressed by it when I heard one door after another opening and closing outside, away from the main corridor. I lowered my racket. In my imagination, I followed the sounds through the corridors until I was inside the Perspex court in the badminton hall.

It was quiet. The Perspex walls were a pale, icy blue.

Now that I was inside them, it seemed to me that the walls, the whole structure, existed outside of time. Here, no one was rushing me, and if I wanted to, I could think. I began to feel my muscles twitching with the traces of another game. I was on the T in the Perspex court calculating my next move, and I was in Court 6, playing. To someone watching, it would seem that I was out of my depth, bewildered, slow getting to the T, and slow to set off. But more often than not, I got to the ball, and even if the shot I played was not perfectly executed and would not cause anyone to break their racket against the wall, it was enough to surprise and wrong-foot my opponent. After twenty minutes, I had her at match point and my mind was buzzing because it wasn't only me playing this girl, it was whatever was in the badminton hall.

When I met Khush and Mona on the stairs, Mona asked me cheerfully what I was thinking. She said that after the first minutes of the match, Pa had said something to Uncle Pavan and gone to sit apart from everyone in the viewing gallery. Then, for twenty minutes he didn't move. He just sat forward and watched me. Mona's voice was like a sliver of glass now, like something broken and sharp. A few times when she looked at Pa, she said, she had been reminded of that man who was eaten by rats. What man? I said, but Mona kept on. At match point, Pa had shot to his feet as if he couldn't help himself and when he finally sat down after the point had been played, it was impossible to tell if he was crying or laughing. If he went mad after this, Mona said, I was responsible. She stopped abruptly on the stairs and said that that wasn't what she meant and I said it was okay. Everything went around and around inside Mona's mind, and I knew, and she knew, that it always would.

Pa was in the gallery above Ged's court, where it was standing room only. He turned. His eyes were tired, but there was a soft light in them and he didn't look mad. I went to stand next to him. For a minute we watched the game in silence. 'Don't do that in the final,' Pa said. His voice was so warm. 'I won't,' I said.

Ged lost his semifinal match. His opponent had been pushing for a long game but Ged hadn't been up for that. His mind hadn't been on the game at all, and he might as well have put his racket down after ten minutes.

On the stairs, he shook his head and smiled briefly. He didn't want to talk about the game. Maybe he wanted me to say something necessary or important, about us, about the future. We faced each other and the sun set at Western Lane and turned the smudges on the walls orange and pink. In the funfair, the sad, sad horse tried to raise its head. 'Uncle Pavan's buying Cokes,' I said dully. Ged looked at me, then nodded as if I had said something better.

In the bar everyone was quiet. It was Maqsud who looked around at all our faces and began to talk. He said no one had imagined I would come this far, and it didn't matter what happened next. I wasn't to worry about it because what mattered was being here. When no one replied he finished his drink, put his glass on the table, and said, 'Still. After all, we're here,' and demanded to know if anyone had seen the other girl play. The other girl was the younger Prince sister, Alexandra. Her matches had happened at the same time as mine so everyone was surprised when Uncle Pavan replied that he had seen her. He regretted it as soon as he mentioned it. 'I only saw a little,' he murmured, but Maqsud wanted more. Uncle Pavan searched around. Turning to me, he knocked over a half-empty glass, his or Pa's. He set it right before it spilled too much. He cleared his throat. 'Don't worry about her,' he said to me. 'You take your time.' Mona choked on her drink, and Khush, red-faced, grabbed my hand and squeezed it quickly. It was exactly what Ma would say to us when she sensed that we were struggling with something, *you take your time*, over her shoulder, eyes shining, face flushed pink from standing over pans of boiling water, and because she spoke so few words to us in English, we could all see her now. We looked at Pa but he just kept staring at the spill in front of him.

In the badminton hall, someone had taken care of things. The floor had been swept clean and neat rows of benches had been set up around the court's perimeter. The court itself rose at least a few inches off the floor, and even under the lights it was glowing, faintly blue.

Pa stopped in the doorway when he saw it.

'What, Pa?' I said.

He adjusted the strings on my racket. 'Your uncle's right,' he replied.

He gave me the racket and put his hand on my shoulder and for a few seconds he let it sit there.

Alexandra was waiting by the benches. We shook hands and the referee reminded us of the rules, and more people entered the hall. Then the hall lights were dimmed.

From inside the Perspex court, we could see out, but indistinctly. It was like seeing out from inside a giant block of ice. We saw shadows and movement. Dark, watery indigos and blues. It seemed to me that Pa was sitting on the front bench on my backhand and my sisters were beside him and Ged was standing up, but I wasn't sure.

The court was freezing inside. Alexandra and I kept our hooded tops zipped and made the most of the warm-up, hitting with pace and running for the ball. We tensed whenever our rackets made contact with the walls. We didn't know if the walls would become scratched, or crack like ice, or if the Perspex would weaken in some way with too many blows.

Alexandra was going to beat me. I believed this from the beginning. She played wide forehand drives to the back of the court and then drop after drop at the front. She didn't hit breathtaking shots but there was something mysterious and relentless about her rhythm, and I was drawn into following her. When she hit a length past the service box, I was bringing my shoulder round and my racket arm was back, ready to do the same, and when she hit a drop it didn't seem to me that she was trying to end a point, rather that she was pulling me in to join her at the front of the court.

Soon I could no longer hear the ball, only our breath and the soft squeak of our shoes on the wood. We moved around one another in near silence. The rallies went on and on and after every point, Alexandra wiped her racket hand swiftly along the wall on her side and I did the same on mine. Maybe Pa was out there trying to tell me to find my own rhythm and break Alexandra's, but it didn't matter because we both knew that if she went on as she was, there was no way I could break her. In the car park, Ged had asked me if I had thought about what would happen after this. I had and I hadn't. I'd imagined as far as Durham and Cleveland, but then there was a wall. Now I was inside the wall, and all I could do was stay in it.

Slowly, outside, close to the Perspex, the shadowy figures on my backhand became more definite. Pa was sitting erect and his face was dark and tense. He was watching Alexandra. He was looking for some weakness in her, and my sisters were watching him. Uncle Pavan was standing far back with Ged. The two of them were just shapes, like hills or mountains in the distance.

At twenty minutes and thirty minutes I was meeting Alexandra shot for shot, and at forty the audience was murmuring because no one had anticipated this. Pa's expression only grew darker and more tense. At forty-five minutes, something changed. Alexandra began hitting fewer lengths and when she did hit a length, she placed the ball high on the front wall. I looked at Pa and we understood at the same moment what was happening: Alexandra was trying to give herself more time. She was tired.

You can think it out, but in the end you don't know what is going to happen until you go through it. I had thought Alexandra would certainly beat me, because it had not occurred to me that if I stayed with her long enough I might simply outlast her. I played a backhand, bringing my shoulder round and swinging my racket as if the wall did not exist. Alexandra played a forehand and when I played another backhand, she followed, and then I was leading. At forty-eight minutes Alexandra was still following, and Pa's hands were fists.

Then I began to flag and lost my first point since taking the lead.

Pa rose to his feet. He took half a step forward. I lost another point, and another. Pa looked hopelessly towards the door of the badminton hall. That man who was eaten by rats. Mona's phrase hovered in my mind but I kept hitting. All I had to do, I thought, was follow Alexandra until I got my second wind, and Pa would see that she had nothing left in her, whereas I did. I stayed close to Alexandra. I hit deep, safe shots. Alexandra played to my backhand because she thought it was weaker and maybe it was. It didn't matter. I won back the serve and this time I didn't lose it.

At fifty-six minutes when I had match point, I glanced out and saw that everything was dark and watery again. I hesitated. I felt my racket arm drop. Ged and Uncle Pavan replied by stepping forward as one, and for a beat I saw them as clearly as if they were standing in front of me, telling me to hold steady. Then they stepped aside, and I let my racket fly.

The serve was good.

Alexandra returned with a drive to my backhand. As I met the ball, I sensed her moving in front of the T because she'd guessed what I was going to do. I did it anyway. I hit a volley drop, soft and controlled – and the ball rolled sweetly, miraculously, out of the nick, and Alexandra didn't even try to get to it. Everyone in the badminton hall stood up.

With the acoustics in the hall, it was like four hundred spectators getting to their feet instead of forty. There was whistling and shouting. I stood on the T, lightheaded and breathless, replaying those last seconds, feeling around me the movement of Alexandra's body, of my own body, of my racket, the displaced air, and then the hit that was so soft and clean, and I saw Maqsud outside, close to the wall, applauding and beaming, and next to him, Uncle Pavan, smiling gently.

Further back, Ged and my sisters were applauding too, but as my attention fell on them, a new feeling came over me. It had to do with disappointment and confusion. It was only gradually that I understood what it was.

Pa was missing from the bench.

On the backhand, where Pa was supposed to be, white scratches lined the wall. I looked at my sisters and they looked back at me, smiling, denying that anything was wrong.

Where had he gone, my father?

I imagined him standing in the corridor beyond the badminton hall. His arms hung at his sides. The beating noise from the badminton hall was faint, but it hurt his ears and it did not occur to him to lift his hands to cover them. That was how I imagined him. If the dog Fourth Avenue entered the corridor at that moment, I thought, with his yellow teeth, and his big shoulders lurching from side to side, he would pass by Pa. He would not even turn his head.

I heard Alexandra saying something over the noise in the hall. She gripped my free hand, held it high in hers, and she indicated that I should hold my racket up, and I did, and the noise brought tears to my eyes.

The hall lights were switched on. With the lights up, I was supposed to come out, and Alexandra was supposed to follow. The crowd went silent when I hovered on the T. I looked out to where my sisters were standing. And then suddenly there he was, my father, in his dark suit, beside my sisters as if he had been there all along. Khush was talking to him and gesturing at the court, and Pa was frowning slightly because somewhere drums were beating, and it was hard for him to hear. I knew that Khush was describing what he had missed. I stood where I was, very slowly adjusting the strings on my racket. Pa had gone out into the corridor because he had thought there was hope and then there wasn't, and he could not bear it. He thought there was nothing he could do in the badminton hall. But it wasn't the badminton hall but the corridor that was the problem for him. Because what was there for him in the corridor? It was empty, it had no use for him, and we, my sisters and I, had put him there. When Khush finished talking, Pa's eyes met mine. I tried to let him know that I needed something from him, but what, what? He straightened. He made an almost imperceptible sign with his hand. It didn't mean anything, it was nothing we had rehearsed. But I checked my grip as if that was what he wanted. Then I nodded to Alexandra, put my racket down, and opened the door.

There was a milky shimmering cloud in a great diagonal across the sky and inside the cloud was a black mouth that also shimmered. Uncle Pavan and I were both staring at the road and the sky as he drove. I wasn't frightened of the black mouth ahead of us because at first I mistook the whole thing for mist, and then Uncle Pavan told me the opposite was true, that the sky was clear now and what we were seeing was gas and dust and light from more than a billion stars. It was our own galaxy, he said, and we were looking at it from inside. We were seeing it as it had been, maybe tens of thousands of years ago, and by now it was possible these stars did not exist.

'But we're seeing them,' I said.

'Yes.'

We were driving north. Maqsud was driving south, and with him Pa and Ged and my sisters.

We had all stood in the car park, shivering, hands deep inside coat pockets. The tournament people had given me a Prince bag and twenty pounds, and my sisters wanted to know what I would do with the money. I didn't know. Ged had been looking after the Prince bag. He handed it to me then. When he looked away, his thick, short lashes cast a shadow under his eyes. He looked different. There was a roughness about him. His jaw and cheekbones were harder than they had been. Here, in the car park, he looked older and I was sure that I did too. We were shy and afraid because there was all this feeling between us and we didn't know who we were.

Mona hugged me and said we would go shopping when they came to visit.

Uncle Pavan looked at Pa. 'Come soon,' he said, and Pa said, 'Yes.'

I thought this must be the same sky that the others would see from Maqsud's car, and maybe they would stop to look. I asked Uncle Pavan if we could stop. I didn't know there was too much light surrounding Maqsud's car, making it impossible for the others to see what we saw. I didn't know that in any case Pa's eyes had been closed for miles, and my sisters weren't looking outside, they were playing cards with Ged and Shaan, all squeezed into the back seat, laughing, making alliances, trying hopelessly to hide their cards from one another, and they were happy, and the sky did not exist.

Uncle Pavan and I sat in our car looking out, and then we drove on.

At home, Uncle Pavan warmed cocoa and we drank it in the kitchen. When Aunt Ranjan came downstairs, she looked exactly as she had looked when we left, and this startled us. Aunt Ranjan asked about our journey. We said it was fine. I showed her my Prince bag. She smiled wearily. She said it was late and I should go to bed.

But she and my uncle stood outside under the balcony of my bedroom until much later, and I knelt above them with my blanket around me. The three of us looked out at the black shapes of the rose arbour, the trees, the railway track. Stars appeared and disappeared. My knees began to ache. Below me, Aunt Ranjan wanted badly to ask Uncle Pavan how things stood now and Uncle Pavan wanted to tell her, but she wasn't sure how to ask and he wasn't sure how to begin. Soon, I thought, it would be morning, and night, and morning again, and it wouldn't matter, except to someone watching from so far off that they couldn't know yet.

Uncle Pavan began slowly. Since he did not know how to make what he had to say mean something to Aunt Ranjan, he described everything. He described it all as if it had happened long ago, as if we had leapt forward in time, and decades had passed since we had stood with Pa on the bridge with the lights blinking, remembering Jahangir Khan and Gogi Alauddin and Qamar Zaman. As if, when it came to squash, it was already no longer all about the Pakistanis, but the Egyptians playing inside a glass court at the foot of the Pyramids.

Taking his time, Uncle Pavan spoke of Pa, and I felt Pa's presence strongly. He spoke of Ged, and very softly my palm trembled. In his own way, my uncle hunted for markers, looked for beginnings and progressions, things for the mind to snag on. He was careful, always, when it came to the subject of Ma, and Aunt Ranjan was grateful because it was for both brothers, not only Pa but Uncle Pavan too, that Ma had come first. For Uncle Pavan it was a deep love that he could not place, the love for a sister, or a friend to his soul, why should he have to say? For my aunt, this part was difficult. It seemed to my aunt impossible for her to come close to Ma in anything. And so, Uncle Pavan trod with care, and Aunt Ranjan felt it, and understood that this care itself was love. Once or twice, Pa looked up from the electric heater or the television he was mending for one neighbour or another, as if he knew that four hundred miles away Uncle Pavan's subject was Ma and he wanted to be part of it, but he lowered his head quickly because he understood this was not about him. My father stood to one side, and back and forth between my aunt and uncle the days went, and for a time, for how long I don't remember, something glowed very faintly beyond the trees. It glowed and disappeared. Then, because he was tired, my uncle's voice began to drift, and his breath froze, and I stood up.

Acknowledgements

My warmest thanks:

To Tracy Bohan, Mitzi Angel, Ravi Mirchandani, Martha Kanya-Forstner, Jacqueline Ko, Jennifer Bernstein, Milo Walls, Lauren Roberts, Rodrigo Corral, Camilla Elworthy, Emma Bravo, Roshani Moorjani, Marta Catalano, Moesha Parirenyatwa, Lynn Henry, Hilary Lo and all at the Wylie Agency, FSG, Picador and Knopf Canada.

To Tom Morris, Sally O'Reilly, Hannah Vincent, Paula Greco, Jacinta Mulders, Brendan Barrington, Danny Denton, Amanda Austen, Rob Saunders, Tom Horner, Emma Cummins, Marie Gethins, Gillian Watson, Claire Adam, Molly Strauss, Kevin Murphy, Maggie Gee, Evelyn Somers, Claire Keegan, 88 and the Stinging Fly Summer School.

For their writing about squash, I'm indebted to Jahangir Khan, Rahmat Khan and Richard Eaton (*Winning Squash*), Jonah Barrington (*Murder in the Squash Court*), Rod Gilmour and Alan Thatcher (*Jahangir Khan 555*) and James Willstrop (*Shot and a Ghost*). And thank you to Peter Walker, Peter Genever, Andrew Shelley and the World Squash Library.

To my family and friends.

To Graeme.